Nc

Sean st

h

P Wh

iR

FM

"It'll

"Oka

He

it in

"Yo

"Th

roo

"Yo

in t

som

sha

"Do

Sea

run

"Yo

"No

Sea

Books by Ron and Janet Benrey

Love Inspired Suspense

Glory Be! #55
Gone to Glory #67
Grits and Glory #110

RON AND JANET BENREY

began writing romantic cozy mysteries together more than ten years ago—chiefly because they both loved to read them. Their successful collaboration surprised them both, because they have remarkably different backgrounds.

Ron holds degrees in engineering, management and law. He built a successful career as a nonfiction writer specializing in speechwriting and other aspects of business writing. Janet was an entrepreneur before she earned a degree in communications, working in such fields as professional photography, executive recruiting and sporting-goods marketing.

How do they write together and still stay married? That's the question that readers ask most. The answer is that they've developed a process for writing novels that makes optimum use of their individual talents. Perhaps even more important, their love for cozy mysteries transcends the inevitable squabbles when they write one.

Ron & Janet Benrey

Grits and Glory

Steeple Hill®

Published by Steeple Hill Books™

STEEPLE HILL BOOKS

Steeple
Hill®

ISBN-13: 978-0-373-44300-0
ISBN-10:   0-373-44300-5

GRITS AND GLORY

www.SteepleHill.com

Printed in U.S.A.

Forget the former things; do not dwell on the past.
—*Isaiah* 43:18

Forget the former things; do not dwell on the past.

Isaiah 43:18 NIV

ONE

"I am the administrator of Glory Community Church, gentlemen."

Ann Trask sat upright in her chair and spoke with determination. She hoped the rigid posture would make her look more formidable. "It is *my* responsibility to remain in the building in the event of an emergency—especially when Pastor Hartman is out of town."

One of the two big men standing in front of Ann's desk grinned at her. Rafe Neilson, Glory's deputy police chief, was solidly in her corner. The other man scowled and made a disparaging gesture.

"We don't need false bravery today, Miss Trask. There's a major hurricane bearing down on our corner of North Carolina. Gilda is the proverbial 'really big one,' a mid-September wind machine strong enough to be a killer. Her outer rain bands are flooding Glory's streets as we speak." Phil Meade's gaze locked onto Ann's face as he spoke directly to her. "The outer rain bands are on the periphery of the storm, but they sometimes spawn tornadoes along with the drenching rain. They're a taste of what's to come. You don't want to be here when the main storm arrives." He crossed his arms. "I say that as Glory's director of emergency management."

Ann took a deep breath and prayed that neither man could hear her heart thumping. She knew to the depths of her queasy stomach that Phil Meade—a respected expert in disaster management—had spoken the truth. He even looked the part: late forties, tall, wide, florid-faced and gray at the temples, with a powerful bass voice that commanded respect. But right as Phil was, she couldn't run away. Not again. This time, she would take control of her fears.

"What do you think, Rafe?" Ann said, as evenly as she could. She noted that he had stopped grinning.

Please don't let Rafe side with Phil against me.

"Well, we all agree that Glory Community Church is one of the most solidly built structures in town. Moreover, it's located on the highest patch of ground we have. That's why we've designated it as an emergency shelter. If there's anyplace in Glory that can survive a major hurricane, this is it."

"Exactly—" Ann began, but Rafe kept talking.

"However, I feel uneasy that you'll remain when virtually everyone else has evacuated Glory."

"*Dozens* of people are staying," she protested.

Phil Meade jumped back in. "Correct! Police officers, firefighters, a few medical professionals, the mayor, my staff, a handful of other essential personnel, and me." He pointed at Ann. "We don't need a twenty-four-year-old *civilian* putting her life at risk and making our work more difficult."

"I'm almost twenty-five, Mr. Meade. There are younger police officers patrolling Glory, and some of them have spouses and children to worry about. I'm single—free as the proverbial bird. I don't even have my mother to take care of. She's across the state visiting my brother in Asheville." Ann took a swift breath. "Someone has to be on duty in Glory's emergency shelter—I'm glad for the opportunity to be useful."

Phil turned to Rafe. "What are we going to do about this?"

"I'd have to put her in handcuffs to make her leave town." He clapped Phil on the shoulder. "Like she said, someone needs to be on duty inside the church."

"*Pah!* You deal with her. I have sensible people to worry about." Phil strode toward the door to Ann's office, and then spun around. "Miss Trask, make sure you give Rafe a phone number for your next of kin. Just in case."

Ann camouflaged the jolt of anxiety she felt with a hollow laugh while she listened to Phil's boot-shod feet clomp down the church's hallway. He had said the perfect thing to push her panic button.

Please don't make my mother deal with another visit from the police.

"Phil has a point," Rafe said. "This may not be the wisest decision you've made."

"Perhaps not." Ann swallowed hard to clear the alarm from her voice. "But I have an important job to do."

And this time people are going to see me do it properly.

"Well, if your mind is made up—"

"Good!" Ann said quickly. "Now that that's settled, when will things get bad in Glory?"

Rafe's expression became grim. "Gilda's eye wall—and her strongest winds—will reach Glory at five o'clock this afternoon."

"So the worst of the hurricane should be over before nightfall, right?"

"I'm afraid not. Gilda's a massive storm. Her remnants could be with us until the wee hours of tomorrow morning."

"Do you think the electricity will fail?"

Rafe nodded. "Everyone at the emergency command center expects the power to fail a few minutes after Gilda hits. The citizens of Glory should be prepared to spend Monday night in the dark." He smiled. "Correction! Most of us should. The church, however, has an emergency generator that will switch on automatically. You'll be a beacon of light for the rest of Glory."

"That's part of every church's job description."

Rafe uttered a soft grunt of agreement, then asked, "Are any volunteers still working in the church?"

"No," Ann said. "They're all gone. They hung the storm shutters early this morning and finished installing the plywood panels over our stained-glass windows about a half hour ago." She made a vague gesture toward her own shuttered window. "It's as dark as a tomb inside the sanctuary."

"Tombs survive big hurricanes. Anyway, I'm glad the volunteers are finished."

"Me, too," Ann said, although she'd been sorry to see the eight men go. They hadn't even taken time to say goodbye. Seconds after the hammering stopped, Ann heard eight engines rev. She understood completely. The volunteers had to protect their own homes from the approaching storm and then evacuate their families further inland, at least to Rocky Mount, perhaps to Winston-Salem.

"I see you're wearing the miniature tactical police radio I gave you," Rafe said.

Ann tugged at the two lanyards around her neck. She felt the small lozenge-shaped gizmo bounce against her chest. "I keep the radio you gave me next to my high-intensity flashlight."

"Our emergency command center is part of police headquarters, less than three blocks from the church. Contact me if you need any help."

Ann bit her tongue. She wanted to say, *You can count on it.* Instead, she said, "I won't need any help. The church is fully battened down."

The building became astonishingly silent after Rafe said his goodbyes and left. Ann could hear the quartz clock on her desk counting off the seconds. The ticking sound seemed louder than it ever had before, and somehow threatening.

"The church is one of the most solidly built structures in Glory," she reminded herself again. "Gilda can huff, puff, and tear loose a few roof shingles, but the walls won't fall down. And the church's generator will keep the lights on all night.

You don't have anything to worry about. So stop worrying. This isn't going to be like last time. I'm much better prepared.

"We've got trouble," Sean Miller said to the person he thought was seated right behind him. "I can't find a safe place to park the broadcast van." When he received no response, he looked around and saw that Carlo Vaughn had moved to the back of the van and was rummaging through the closet.

Sean ignored the rush of exasperation that made him want to throw something. "Carlo, *please* pay attention. I said that we don't have a home for the van."

"I heard you, but I have a more pressing problem to solve. I don't know which of my waterproof rain suits to wear this afternoon. The yellow looks good on me, but I hate the oversized Storm Channel logo embroidered on the front and the back."

"Then put on your red suit."

"It pinches at the waist, and the hood is less flattering."

"What about the navy-blue slicker?"

"Blue is too dark during a heavy storm. My torso disappears—I end up looking like someone removed my head from my body."

"Don't give me any ideas," Sean muttered under his breath. Then he said, "Our *only* pressing problem right now is finding a parking place for the broadcast van. You're scheduled to go live in less than an hour. I can't set up the camera and the lights, start our generator, or get the satellite antenna working until we're safely parked."

Carlo returned to Sean's cramped workstation. "I thought you planned to park behind the high school."

Sean poked his index finger at the map of Glory he'd taped to the desktop. "That was okay before Gilda took direct aim at the town. The high school is located in a low spot that's likely to flood."

"You think so?"

"I know so."

Carlo frowned. "What about that other parking spot we scouted this morning?"

"The local cops called me five minutes ago. The parking structure at Glory Regional Hospital is no longer available because the town is going to use it as a staging area for emergency vehicles."

"It's *your* job to bed down the van. I'm confident that you'll find a solution," Carlo said, heading back to the closet.

"I see one remaining possibility on the map—the parking lot next to Glory Community Church. It's sizable and not likely to flood."

"Problem solved! We'll park at the church. I don't

understand why you're making such a big deal about a simple decision."

"The decision may be simple, but the church is private property and we don't have permission to operate from their parking lot."

"Then we'd better get over there and ask."

"Gee, why didn't I think of that?" Sean fought to keep his voice even. The cardinal rule of remote broadcasting was don't upset the "talent" an hour before an upcoming broadcast.

"I don't have any choice," Carlo said glumly. "I'll have to make do with the red jacket."

"Poor baby!" Sean muttered.

"But it's really too bad we don't have a green rain jacket. I look great in green."

Sean swallowed another sigh. "Let's go visit the church."

God, if you're listening, please turn Carlo into a frog. He does look great in green.

Ann couldn't see outside but she could hear the wind-blown rain drumming on the heavily shuttered windows and it was getting louder by the minute. She wished that she knew more about extreme weather. How could she estimate the amount of rain falling? How much wind did it take to peel shingles off the roof? What should she do if the lights failed inside the church?

Stop worrying about Gilda. Other people in Glory are in much greater danger than you are.

The sound of the church's doorbell promptly switched her thoughts. *Maybe someone wants to take refuge inside the church?* Ann raced to front door. She had to push the brass handle with all of her strength to keep the stout wooden door ajar against the force of the wind. A yellow hood poked around the edge of the door.

"May we come in?" said a male voice.

"Of course. But I don't dare let go of the door."

"We'll work the door. Stand back so you don't get soaked. It's like the bottom of Niagara Falls out here."

Ann stepped sideways. Mr. Yellow Suit and a taller man dressed in a red rain slicker and pants slipped into the narthex and pulled the door shut. Ann recognized the red-suited man straight away when he tugged back his hood. Carlo Vaughn was the Storm Channel's star weather reporter. She couldn't help staring at him. The man was drop-dead gorgeous: a classic chiseled face, perfect features, lovely chestnut-colored hair that framed his brow, glowing dark brown eyes, and a smile that lit up the narthex.

"Good afternoon," Mr. Yellow Suit said. "We're from the Storm Channel."

Ann responded to his greeting politely, then looked back at Carlo to take in more details: the powerful aura of self-assurance he projected…his brilliant, dazzling smile… the absence of a wedding ring on his third finger…

"My name is Carlo Vaughn." Carlo's voice oozed like warm syrup over a buttered waffle. He gave his name a slightly European pronunciation, hitting the second syllable rather than the first.

"Welcome to Glory Community Church," she replied. "I've seen you on TV many times."

"I've come to Glory because there's a hurricane on the way."

"'Storms come, storms go. We follow the storms,'" Ann said.

"You even know our slogan." He extended a hand. "And your name is?"

"Ann Trask," she managed, trying to conceal her excitement.

"Well, Ann Trask, I have a favor to ask of you. May we locate our broadcast van in your parking lot?" He pointed toward the rear of the building.

"Our van is completely self-contained," Mr. Yellow Suit barked.

"Thank you, Sean," Carlo said. "Ann, let me introduce Sean Miller. Sean is my associate, the man behind the camera."

Ann studied Sean. He'd pulled back his hood, revealing a plain face that currently overflowed with annoyed impatience. His lack of good looks compared to Carlo—plus his sour expression—worked together to create a bad impression. She found herself feeling annoyed at this boorish hanger-on.

"It's a pleasure to meet you, ma'am," Sean said perfunctorily. "The fact is, your parking lot may be the only dry ground in Glory when Gilda hits. We have a broadcast scheduled in less than forty-five minutes. May we park in your lot?"

Ann returned her gaze to Carlo. "How big is your van?"

"Imagine a bread delivery truck with a satellite dish on the roof. We'll find an out-of-the-way location in the back—you won't even know we're there."

"That won't be necessary, Mr. Vaughn."

"Please call me Carlo."

"Well, Carlo," Ann said, feeling a flush in her cheeks, "park as close to the church as you'd like. This is one of the most solidly built structures in Glory. We're set up as an emergency shelter—come inside whenever you need to. Our side entrance faces the parking lot."

"That's *very* kind of you."

Ann noticed that Sean rolled his eyes. She wondered

how a gentleman like Carlo could spend his days traveling with an ill-mannered assistant who clearly lacked his boss's sophistication and polish.

"Ann, I have to get ready to go on the air," Carlo said. "I'll leave Sean here to work out the details. Let's chat later, after my broadcast."

"That would be great," Ann said, smiling.

She took a step backward as Sean eased the front door open for Carlo, allowing a whirlwind of raindrops to spray the narthex. Carlo gave a jaunty wave and marched into the downpour. Sean seemed to be shaking his head as he pulled the heavy door shut.

Ann suddenly realized she'd met a TV star while wearing an abysmal outfit—an old pair of blue jeans, a scruffy plaid shirt and bright yellow plastic clogs. What little makeup she had put on that morning had certainly worn off. *Why not spruce up before Carlo comes back?*

Why not, indeed?

"Ms. Trask," Sean said loudly, "I'm on a tight schedule."

She tried not to frown at his unpleasant attempt to catch her attention. "Certainly. What do you need from me?"

"I wanted to explain that I intend to park the van in the lee of the church. That way, the building will shield the van from the worst of the winds but our satellite antenna will still have an unobstructed view of the sky."

"Whatever you decide is fine with me."

"There's a small downside to parking so close to the church. You'll probably hear our generator from time to time."

"Oh, you have a generator? We have one, too."

"My condolences." He shook his head gloomily. "Ours is the thing I hate most in the world. It's ornery and unreliable—and a pain to start."

"Unreliable? Is that common for generators?"

"Usually," Sean said.

"I'm relying on our generator to work if the power quits tonight," Ann said, trying not to panic.

Sean looked at her closely. "Sorry. I shouldn't have made an offhand comment. You probably have a heavy-duty commercial model that starts automatically in the event of a power failure."

"I don't know what we have, only that there's a large gray steel cabinet behind the church."

"Well, I'd better get back to van. I have less than thirty minutes to put Carlo on the air."

Ann forced her frown into a smile. "I know you're busy, Sean, but before you go, could you do me a favor?"

He peered at her uncertainly. "If I can."

"Look, you seem to understand generators. Would you help me make sure that ours is okay?"

He glanced at his watch. "Well, I suppose I can give you two minutes. Take me to the generator control panel."

"Control panel?" She hoped that she looked less bewildered than she sounded.

"A small metal box with buttons and lights." He looked at his watch again. "Maybe I should come back later."

Ann fought back a touch of distress she didn't want Sean to see.

"No need. I know what you're talking about. It's hanging on the wall in the utility room."

She quickly led Sean to the control panel. He took a moment to examine it. "Who's Richard Squires?"

"One of our members—why?"

"There's a note on the wall. 'In case of a problem with the generator, call Richard Squires.'"

"Is there a problem?"

"We're about to find out. The generator is set to automatic, but you can test it by pushing the red manual start button."

Ann pushed the red button. Almost immediately, she heard a growling noise outside, then the reassuring rumble of an engine. Three small indicator lights on the control panel began to glow green.

"The engine's running fine, there's plenty of fuel, and the system is producing electricity."

"Great!" Ann said, full of relief.

"Hit the black button to turn it off," Sean said.

But before Ann could lift her hand, the middle light began to flash red. A second later, the engine quit.

"What's wrong?" she asked.

"According to the indicator light, something in the fuel system."

"Can you fix it?"

"I'm sorry. I don't even have time to try. We go on the air in a few minutes. Perhaps you should call this Richard Squires guy on the note."

Ann immediately felt foolish for not thinking of Richard herself. "Good idea. I'll call Richard. He's the church volunteer in charge of the generator."

"I need to get back to our van."

"Thank you. You've been very helpful."

"I'll see myself out."

"Be careful out there," she said, reaching for the cell phone in her pocket.

The generator is Richard Squires's baby. He'll know what to do.

TWO

Sean studied the pewter-colored but rainless sky. The break between rain bands gave him a small window of time to deploy the lights and camera. Everything should be fine unless there was an unexpected problem with the camera's focus and color balance.

I could encourage the unlikely to happen and Carlo would never know.

Sean pushed the delightfully evil thought out of his mind. He would do his job properly, even though he ached to make Carlo look like a fuzzy, multicolored blob. Sean finished setting up with four minutes to spare. He found Carlo in the back of the van memorizing a script he'd written on a yellow notepad.

"Everything's ready for you," Sean said.

Carlo looked up and smirked. "Kind of like blond little-miss-what's-her-name."

"If you're talking about the woman in the church, her name is Ann Trask."

"So it is." He chortled. "She's not up to my usual standards, of course, but one can't be choosy during a hurricane."

"This isn't spring break, Carlo. You're in Glory on assignment, remember?"

"An assignment in a hick city is a perfect opportunity for a quick encounter with a local lass."

"Ann Trask doesn't seem a 'quick encounter' type of woman."

"Says who? She checked out my ring finger, I checked out hers. Didn't you spot her come-hither look when she saw me?"

"That's nonsense!"

"There's nothing like stormy weather to relax a woman's inhibitions, if you know what I mean."

"I do know what you mean—and you're making me angry."

Carlo snorted. "You sound as if you like her."

"What if I do?"

"Great! We'll both court her. Competition increases the joy of victory," said Carlo.

Sean flinched as a bolt of lightning illuminated the interior of the van. The thunderclap came less than a second later.

"That was close," Carlo said. "Since when do hurricanes have lightning?"

"Most don't. Gilda is a special storm."

"Which means?"

"Her vertical wind flows are creating an electrical field. That's unusual."

"Unusual *bad?* Or unusual *good?*" Carlo's normally melodious voice had become a little shrill.

"I don't know."

"You have to know. You're the expert. You actually have a degree in meteorology."

"Don't get your rain pants in a twist. Lightning doesn't make a hurricane more powerful."

"But it definitely increases the danger to reporters

broadcasting from parking lots. I'm not in the mood to get struck by lightning this afternoon."

"We're parked next to a tall aluminum light pole. If lightning hits anything around here, it will be that."

"Are you sure?"

"Completely." He pointed toward the door. "Now get out there. We go live in two minutes."

Sean sat down at his workstation and manipulated the joysticks that controlled the TV camera and the lights. He slipped his headset over his ears, pushed the attached microphone close to his mouth, and spoke to Cathy McCabe at the Storm Channel's broadcast headquarters on Long Island.

"Hi, Cathy. We're ready in Glory."

"Glad to hear it," she replied. "How's Gilda so far?"

"Wet, windy and electric. Mr. Magnificent is worried about being zapped by lightning."

"Get a picture if it happens. I know a dozen women who'd want copies." Cathy's voice became cool and businesslike. "Switching to Carlo in twenty seconds."

Sean pushed the button that connected his microphone to Carlo's earpiece. "Cue in fifteen seconds."

Sean heard Carlo clear his throat. "Four…three…two…" Sean counted softly.

A red light lit on his console, confirming that an identical light on the camera had signaled Carlo to begin. Sean studied the monitor screen as Carlo spoke into his handheld microphone. As usual, the camera loved Carlo. He looked artlessly elegant even though his jacket's tunnel-like hood was fully extended to keep his face dry.

"This is Carlo Vaughn reporting from Glory, North Carolina. It is only four in the afternoon, but the sky is dark in this pretty waterfront town on the Albemarle Sound, an ominous sign of things to come. Another of Gilda's outer rain bands is dumping precipitation on Glory."

A gust of wind suddenly tugged at Carlo's hood and he grabbed at it with his free hand.

"Most of Glory's six thousand residents have moved to higher ground, leaving a handful of emergency personnel to deal with the approaching hurricane. They've been told to prepare for major damage.

"Gilda is the most powerful hurricane to threaten the Albemarle region in more than a decade. The current forecast predicts steady winds exceeding one hundred miles per hour when Gilda arrives in Glory less than an hour from now."

Sean adjusted the image when a lightning flash illuminated the sky behind Carlo's head. A moment later, the rumble of thunder shook the van. Carlo took the interruption in stride. "As you've just seen and heard, Gilda is also an electrical storm, which is unusual for a hurricane."

"Off in thirty seconds," Sean informed Carlo softly.

Carlo unexpectedly took a sideways step. He gazed at the sky to his left and his right, as if he were an expert meteorologist studying the storm. Sean worked the joystick to move the lens to keep Carlo's face framed in the image. But then, without warning, Carlo stepped closer to the camera, his expression full of compassion and concern. Sean suddenly realized that Carlo was trying to impress Ann Trask.

Cathy's voice filled Sean's headphone. "What's your boy doing? It looks like he's trying to climb into the viewers' laps."

"You don't want to know," Sean said grimly.

Carlo began to speak. "The small cadre of people who chose to remain in Glory will soon be tested by Gilda's fury. I call them the courageous few.

"We're broadcasting from the parking lot of a church that may provide emergency shelter when the storm hits. The person on duty inside—a young woman named Ann Trask—is willing to brave the danger, not for personal gain, but in the spirit of public service. Stay tuned—we'll hear Ms. Trask's observations about Gilda during our next broadcast.

"Glory—we're with you. This is Carlo Vaughn signing off for now."

Sean killed the connection to the TV camera.

Blast the man! He put a phony quiver in his voice and his eyes looked weepy.

Sean poked angrily at more buttons on his control console. It wouldn't matter to Ann that Carlo knew next to nothing about the weather. She wouldn't care that he was merely *imitating* a knowledgeable meteorologist. Nope! Like every other female with a pulse, she'd be dazzled by his smarmy good looks. Sean sighed as he zipped up his jacket and prepared to go outside to retrieve the camera and tripod.

Ann Trask is a grown woman. She'll have to fend for herself in Carlo-land.

"Perhaps I shouldn't say this," Ann said, "but I'm delighted you stayed in town this evening." She positioned a golf umbrella to shield Richard Squires's back from driving rain, fighting against the wind. His big-brimmed baseball cap seemed to be doing a good job keeping rain off his face.

"They won't let me leave Glory," he said with a laugh. "I manage the crew that keeps the rest of the emergency personnel well fed. More light on the right side of the engine, please."

Ann shifted the powerful utility light she held in her

other hand and wished she could do more to help Richard. He was a self-taught expert on engine maintenance and a restorer of vintage cars when he wasn't managing Squires' Place, one of Glory's best restaurants. He also sang tenor in Glory Community's choir.

He picked up a wrench. "One of these days, we'll have to buy a replacement fuel pump, but this fix will keep the engine running throughout Gilda's visit."

"Amen!" Ann murmured.

He went on, "I'm glad that TV fellow tested the generator—I should have done it this morning."

"You're one of our most valuable volunteers, Richard. I thank you for all you do for the church."

She watched Richard stretch to work on the back of the engine. "This is one of those times I wish I was taller," he said. Even standing on a step stool, Richard, who was only an inch or two taller than Ann, had difficulty reaching deep into the generator's cabinet.

Her cell phone rang.

"Give me the utility light," Richard said. "That'll free up your right hand."

Ann managed to flip her phone open and was surprised to find her brother calling.

"Alan! Everything all right with Mom?" she asked.

"Mom's fine—and proud as punch."

"About?"

"You didn't hear it?"

"Hear what?"

"You're famous! Carlo Vaughn talked about you on the Storm Channel."

"Oh, no! What did he say?" Ann laughed.

"He called you one of the 'courageous few.' Even better—he's going to put you on the air later today."

"I've never been on TV before." Ann saw Richard struggling with the utility light and the wrench. "I have to run, Alan. Thanks for the news! I'll call you later. Love to Mom."

Richard extracted himself from the generator box. "I only heard one side of your conversation, but it seems to me that you should find yourself a TV set. The Storm Channel often repeats Carlo Vaughn's broadcasts."

"You don't mind?"

"Not at all. I'm nearly done. I can replace the generator cover by myself."

"Then what will you do, Richard? The storm's getting worse," Ann said, raising her voice to be heard over the wind.

"It's a short drive to the emergency command center. I'll be there long before Gilda arrives for real."

Ann thanked Richard and headed for the Chapman Lounge, the location of the church's only TV set. As she walked down the hallway, she caught a glimpse of her reflection in a glass-paneled door. Nothing about her face appearance had improved during the past hour. *I'd better freshen up if Carlo is going to stand me in front of a TV camera and ask questions.* She made a detour to her office and retrieved the duffel bag she'd packed that morning.

The Chapman Lounge was a comfortable room next to the pastor's office that had a small sofa, two armchairs, and a big-screen TV set. Ann had to wait less than ten minutes for the rerun of Carlo's report.

She felt somewhat eccentric laughing out loud in an empty church, but she couldn't stop herself. Hearing herself praised by Carlo cracked her up. He'd made a grim day more cheery by pushing Gilda to the back of her mind.

She unzipped the duffel bag and surveyed her meager

wardrobe. Everything fell into the "working clothing" category—clothes suitable for working in the kitchen, working in the basement, working on the church grounds. Nothing was really appropriate for a TV interview. She finally decided on a pair of tan chinos (clean but threadbare) and a dark blue cotton sweater (originally part of her mother's wardrobe and at least fifteen years old). The bright blue tactical police radio hanging from the lanyard around her neck would spruce up her outfit with an extra touch of color. It was the best she could do on short notice, she decided.

Ann hadn't meant to stay in the lounge for long, but she got caught up in the Storm Channel's coverage of Gilda provided by other weather reporters who were based closer to North Carolina's Atlantic Coast. The slowly changing satellite images showed the revolving hurricane approaching the shoreline like a huge Frisbee.

Suddenly, the lights flickered. *Not the electricity. Not yet.* They flickered again, then died, leaving the lounge in complete darkness.

Ann fumbled for the flashlight on her lanyard. The lounge, now illuminated by a single beam, seemed bleak and forbidding, a sensation made even worse by the roar of the wind and the pelting of rain against the wooden shutters, sounds previously covered by the TV. Gilda had arrived.

She soon began to hear the reassuring chug of the church's generator. The lights blinked back on.

Please, God, keep the engine going.

Ann decided to move to the narthex, to be closer to the front door. As she walked down the hallway, strange creaks from above added to the cacophony of sound. A few seconds later, a loud tearing noise made her flinch, followed quickly by a loud crash outside. It took her a moment to put the sounds together.

Gilda ripped our steeple off the roof.

Sean stumbled against the wind and managed to grab the handle of Glory Community's door with his good left hand. He used his aching right hand to wipe rain-diluted blood off his face, then gingerly placed his thumb on the doorbell. He pulled again and again, ignoring the throbbing in his head and the haze that seemed to saturate his mind.

He saw the door begin to open and pulled even harder. "It'll take both of us to hold it against the wind," he shouted.

"Okay," Ann shouted back. "You pull, I'll push."

The force of the wind against the heavy steel door was even greater than he'd anticipated. It shoved him a step backward and simultaneously tugged Ann beyond the sill, exposing her to the curtain of rain whirling beneath the narrow overhanging portico. He managed to stay on his feet and, with Ann's help, held the door half-open against a sudden gust.

"Goodness!" she said. "Your head is bleeding."

"The church's steeple fell on our truck when it blew off the roof."

"Where's Carlo?"

"Still in the truck. He's unconscious."

He heard her gasp.

"Let's get inside," he said. "Then I'll call for help."

Sean maneuvered around Ann and grabbed the inside handle. Slowly...*slowly,* they dragged the door shut. Sean felt muzzy headed. He sagged against the wall.

"You need a doctor," she said.

"Probably—but not as much as Carlo."

Ann guided him toward a chair in the small lobby. "You rest. I'll radio the emergency command center."

"I don't want to drip blood on your upholstery."

"That chair has survived a dozen Vacation Bible Schools. It's seen far worse than a few drops of blood."

Sean sat down. He heard the radio crackle, heard Ann say something, but couldn't make out what she said.

He felt Ann shake his shoulder. "Huh?"

"They told me to keep you awake," she said.

He pushed himself to his feet. "I'd better look after Carlo."

"You did that by walking from the parking lot to the church." She pushed him back down. "When you rang the bell, I was already at the side door. I heard the steeple fall and I wanted to see what happened."

"What happened is that it hit our van, and some big pieces of wood plowed through our windshield." Sean recalled the noise of glass breaking…

"Don't fall asleep," Ann said. "Keep talking."

"Carlo and I were sitting up front, watching the storm. I'd lowered the outriggers, so the wind wouldn't tip the van…"

"And?"

"There were two strong gusts. The first one knocked out the electricity. The second made a big 'boom,' glass and wood flying everywhere. Carlo got the worst of it. He was in the passenger seat."

Ann said something into her radio, but he only caught one word: paramedic.

"You're drifting," Ann said. "Stay with me."

"I want apologize on behalf of the Storm Channel."

"Apologize for what?"

"You won't be on television tonight. Our satellite antenna is smashed. No more live broadcasts from Glory."

"And here I went to all the trouble of acquiring this soaking wet look."

Sean gazed at Ann. Her hair was drenched and makeup had run down her cheeks.

"You're pretty."

"Now I'm sure that you need medical attention."

Sean knew he had chuckled, but he couldn't remember what was funny.

He felt another shake. "Talk some more. Tell me about Gilda."

"There's not much to tell. She zigged to the east."

"What does that mean?"

Sean couldn't remember. He told himself to focus. His thoughts abruptly sharpened. "Gilda's track shifted, so Glory's out of the bull's-eye. The storm's weaker southwestern quadrant is blowing through town. The last time I checked, the wind speed was down to eighty-five miles per hour."

"Glory won't be flattened?"

"Nope. There'll be less wind damage and a much smaller storm surge."

"That's the best news I've heard all day," Ann said.

"We weather forecasters try to please."

He watched Ann step away from him when a man dressed in yellow magically appeared at his side.

"This must be our patient," the man said.

Ann nodded. "Sean, meet Dave. He's an emergency medical technician."

Sean tried to look at Dave, but all he could see was a bright light shining in his right eye.

"He might have a concussion," Dave said. "I'll transport him to the hospital, too. Trouble is I can't use a gurney right now because the rest of the team is working on Carlo Vaughn." The light blinked off. "Sean, do you think you can walk to the ambulance?"

"Absolutely!" Sean began to stand—and staggered into Ann.

"Not so fast," Dave said. "I'll support your right side. Ann, you grab his left arm." He continued, "Sean, take a step at a time. Tell us if you feel faint."

"How's Carlo?" Ann asked.

"Yeah," Sean muttered. "How is Carlo?"

"He's conscious, but barely."

"Oh, my!" Ann said.

"Oh, my," Sean echoed, and then he said, "I feel dizzy."

"That's what happens when you get whacked in the head." Dave spoke to Ann. "I'll handle the door, you prop up Sean."

"Yummy!" Sean said when he felt the rain against his face. He lifted his head. The light poles were dark but three powerful floodlights on the ambulance provided enough illumination to see most of the parking lot. The ambulance was positioned on the left side of the van—the side away from the fallen steeple. The wind was still roaring, but less loudly than before.

"Sheesh!" Sean said to Ann. "Your steeple looks like a stack of firewood." He tried to move toward the pile of rubble.

"Slow down," Dave said. "Take one step at a time."

"I must be seeing things in the dark," Ann said. "Don't those look like red boots sticking out from beneath the white boards?"

"Yep," Sean said. "They look exactly like fake boots."

"Except…" Ann began, then went silent.

Dave took over. "Except those are real boots, attached to real legs. Someone else was hit by the falling steeple."

Sean felt uneasy when Ann left his side, ran toward the mound of shattered wood and began to yank the boards away.

"Be careful!" Dave shouted. "Those boards are studded with nails."

"Shouldn't you help her?" Sean said to Dave.

"I will—after I get you to the ambulance."

They'd reached the back of the broadcast van when Ann screamed, loudly enough for Sean to hear her over the wind.

"Dave! It's Richard Squires!"

Sean remembered. *The man who fixes generators...*

And then everything went black.

THREE

Ann stood behind Dave as he kneeled down and felt for the artery in Richard Squires's neck. She knew Dave wouldn't find a pulse. The way Richard's body lay under the shattered boards and the empty expression on his face declared he wasn't alive.

She sucked in two deep breaths to stop the churning in her stomach and glanced up at the clouds that were barely visible against the inky sky. She saw distant flashes of lightning and heard the rumble of faraway thunder.

Both the wind and the rain had subsided considerably since her last sojourn outside, but Gilda was still roaring loudly enough to make conversation difficult without yelling.

"Shift your flashlight a little to the right," Dave shouted. Ann recalled with a shiver that this was the second occasion in less than three hours that she'd held a light for Richard Squires.

Only this time he was dead. All because he had done a good deed for the church and repaired the generator.

She moved her flashlight beam to the right of Richard's head, revealing a glistening pink pool of blood mixed with rainwater. She felt like throwing up but managed to resist the urge. Instead she murmured a quiet prayer asking God to comfort the many people in Glory who knew and liked Richard.

Dave aimed his penlight into Richard's eyes. "No pulse, no pupil response. He's gone." Dave climbed to his feet and added, "Richard must have been walking toward his car over there." Dave pointed toward a compact sedan near the back of the parking lot. Ann could hear the anguish in his voice. "A board smashed the back of his head when the steeple fell."

Ann switched her flashlight off. "Should we—" The question caught in her throat. She tried again. "Should we move him to the ambulance?"

"We don't have a second gurney. I'll come back for Richard's body after I transport Carlo and Sean to the hospital."

The ambulance's rear door was open, the interior brightly lit. Ann could see Carlo, still unconscious, lying on a gurney. A thick white bandage covered his left eye. Sean, his face pale, sat near the door, leaning against another paramedic. The cut on his head had stopped bleeding, but a big bruise on his forehead was beginning to color.

She watched Dave climb into the ambulance. "Do you want to ride with us to the hospital?" he shouted. "You look more than a little shaky yourself."

Ann ached to say yes. She didn't want to be alone inside a sealed-up church—not with Richard Squires lying dead outside, half-buried under a pile of rubble. There was plenty of room for her next to Carlo and Sean. Everyone would understand if she bugged out.

Everyone except Ann Trask. The administrator of Glory Community Church had to stay at her post as long as Gilda threatened the town.

Ann shook her head. "I can't leave."

She expected Dave to argue with her, but he didn't. "It's a short run to the hospital. Expect us back in less than ten minutes." He killed the three floodlights atop the ambulance and yanked the rear door shut. The vehicle's white, red and amber warning signals spun to life, illuminating the jagged remains of the steeple piled next to the Storm Channel's broadcast van and casting bizarre shadows in the parking lot.

Then the ambulance drove away, leaving almost total darkness in its wake. Ann wished that she'd remembered to switch on the exterior light above the church's side door.

She tugged her rain hood forward and tightened the drawstrings. Not that the hood would make much difference. She was soaked to the skin inside her clothing—what were a few more drops of wind-driven rain dripping down her neck?

It hardly made sense to seek a few minutes of shelter inside the church, but she decided to check if anyone had telephoned in her absence. A quick glance at the answering machine in her office told her that no one had called. She made it back to the parking lot in less than five minutes, a moment before one of the police department's four-wheel-drive SUVs, a boxy truck decked out with red and blue strobe lights, entered from King Street. Dave must have notified the emergency command center that Richard had been killed. She cringed. Why hadn't she thought to call Rafe Neilson first?

Probably because you're more shocked by Richard's death than you're willing to admit.

The SUV stopped next to the crippled broadcast van, inches away from Ann. Its headlights lit up the wreckage of the crushed steeple, making Richard's red boots look especially garish compared to the mostly white chunks of smashed wood.

Rafe slipped out of the driver-side door and Phil Meade exited the passenger side. Their faces, alternately lit by blue and red flashes, seemed surreal, but Ann could see anger glowing in Phil's eyes as he strode toward Richard's body.

"Are you okay?" Rafe asked, approaching Ann. Ann took comfort in his strong, caring voice.

"I don't think what's happened has sunk in yet," she said. "It doesn't compute that Richard is dead. He was killed in such a weird way."

"Weird happens," Rafe said, "both for the bad and the good. The broadcast van was in the wrong place at the wrong time. So was Richard Squires. But as far as we know, no one else in town, or the county for that matter, has been seriously injured. One dead and two wounded is a lot better than we hoped for a few hours ago."

"Praise God for that."

Phil's booming voice overpowered the wind. "Praise God indeed for good news, Miss Trask, but *not* for the way that you deal with crises." He brought his face inches from Ann's, close enough for her to see raindrops dribble off his nose. "Your foolish stubbornness killed a wonderful man. I hope you're satisfied."

Ann flinched as the impact of his words hit home. *Phil Meade blamed her for Richard's death.*

She pressed her lips together to control the fury she felt. No way would she give Phil a close-up view of her anger. She would behave like a professional manager, no matter what he said to provoke her.

Rafe stepped between Ann and Phil. "For the tenth time, Phil, you can't blame Ann for Richard's death. She didn't bring down the steeple—that was Gilda's doing. Hurricanes are dangerous. Everyone who stayed in Glory understood the risk. Including Richard Squires."

"For the *eleventh* time," Phil shouted, "there's only one reason that Richard is dead. Ann Trask panicked when she couldn't start the generator, because she's too young and too inexperienced to handle routine problems." He clasped his hands to his temples and shook his head, an extravagantly complex gesture that Ann read as a signal of his bewilderment.

"I don't understand the leaders of Glory Community Church," he said. "Why would you guys put someone in charge of your building during a storm if she can't prime a simple diesel fuel pump?"

Ann felt her anger surge again when Phil spoke about her in the third person, as if she weren't there. She leveled her index finger at him. "Richard kept the generator in good running order. We were supposed to call him immediately if anything went wrong."

"If anything *major* went wrong," Phil replied, with a generous wave of his hands, "or if circumstances truly required the generator to be operational. The very last thing Richard wanted to do this evening was leave his job at the emergency command center and deal with a trivial generator glitch. He did it because you don't know diddly about diesel engines, and because you seemed scared stiff of the dark. That's what he told all of us before he left." He glanced at Rafe. "You were there—you heard Richard moaning and groaning about going to the church. Tell her I'm right."

Ann's anger quickly turned to concern. Rafe's unhappy expression told her that everything Phil had said was true, which meant that Richard's gracious "I should have tested the generator this morning" had been nothing but a polite fib, spoken to cover how he really felt.

That doesn't change my reason for calling him.

Words came rushing out of her mouth.

"I called Richard this evening because I had to. A major hurricane was about to hit Glory. A backup generator is an essential piece of equipment at an emergency shelter. It has to work reliably. The generator was Richard's responsibility, not mine. If he'd maintained it properly, I wouldn't have needed his last-minute help."

Ann watched a vein begin to throb in Phil Meade's temple.

"You're plainly inexperienced," he said angrily, "but I didn't expect you to also be mean-spirited. How dare you blame Richard for your own ineptitude?" He stretched to his full height and went on. "Shame on you! Richard deserves better than that."

Phil spun around and made his way back to Richard's body.

"I give up," Ann said to Rafe. "Phil is determined to blame me."

"Phil's upset about Richard and not in a mood to listen to reason."

She stood still as Rafe gently brushed away a little puddle of rainwater that had collected on the brim of her hood.

"Richard *was* in charge of the generator," Rafe went on. "He often told people that keeping it running was part of his ministry at Glory Community Church."

"Even so, I'd better smooth things over with Phil."

"Good idea," Rafe said, "but give him a chance to calm down before you try. He'll come around after he's had some time to cool off."

Ann knew better. Phil might never "come around." She had embarrassed him earlier by forcing him to back down. He was the sort of person who didn't forgive and forget. Especially not now that he'd discovered her Achilles' heel—her so-called fear of the dark.

"I started my new job at the church just a few months ago," she murmured to herself. "The last thing I need right now is an influential enemy questioning my competence."

God, why do You keep putting me in this position?

Sean felt something squeezing his arm. He opened his eyes and found a smiling nurse standing next to him, pumping a blood pressure cuff. A name tag clipped to her blouse identified her as "Sharon R.N."

"How long have I been out, Sharon?" he asked with a yawn he couldn't suppress.

"Six or seven hours, on and off. The doc stitched the cut on your scalp, ordered an MRI, and then decided you'd suffered nothing worse than a simple concussion and a painful bruise on your forehead. And in case you're wondering why you're yawning, we woke you up repeatedly throughout the night."

Sean glanced at the window behind Sharon. He saw sunlight streaming through the panes and blue, cloudless skies. Gilda had moved on during the night, gifting Glory with a beautiful morning.

Her smile widened. "Are you hungry?"

"Not particularly."

"Blame the concussion. Your stomach might be touchy for a few days. But I do suggest you eat a light breakfast. This could become a busy morning for you. Rafe Neilson wants to talk to you and a woman named Cathy McCabe at the Storm Channel began to call for you an hour ago."

Sean had no idea who Rafe Neilson might be and didn't really care. But Cathy McCabe, his producer, was another matter. "What did you tell her?"

"That I wasn't your secretary and she should leave messages for you on your cell phone. She countered that she didn't much like my attitude and that only an overzealous bureaucrat would refuse to give her any specific information about Carlo's medical status."

Sean chuckled. Like most executive producers, Cathy had a low tolerance for being rebuffed. He imagined the increasingly annoyed tone of her voice. There were a dozen different things she'd want to know—starting with Carlo's health and moving on to the condition of the broadcast van and the pricey camera and control room equipment they carried. He decided not to call her until he had more information.

"What would you say to me if I asked about Carlo's condition?"

"I'd ask you not to give me a hard time. You're not Mr. Vaughn's next of kin, are you?"

"Thankfully no."

"In that case, all I can tell you is what we've told the forty or fifty reporters who've already inquired. We're treating his injuries, which are not life threatening."

She gestured toward an empty bed in the room. "He'll be coming up from the ophthalmological treatment center in a few minutes, and then you can ask him yourself how he's doing. I'm confident that he'll be willing and eager to share."

Sean laughed. "Ah. You discovered that Carlo can be a trifle full of himself."

"A trifle?" She rolled her eyes. "You're a master of understatement this morning. Fortunately, Glory is a gracious town, known for its Carolinian charm and civility. We strive to uphold our reputation even when challenged by an over-inflated northern ego."

Sharon showed him a laminated menu. "Poached egg and some Jell-O for you?"

"Where's the Carolinian charm in that?"

"All of our breakfasts come with grits and a biscuit," she said.

"I stand corrected. Can I take a shower before breakfast?"

"Sure thing—and a stroll down the hallway if you feel up to it. There's a bathrobe hanging behind the bathroom door and paper slippers in the closet. But don't get dressed yet. The doc wants to give you a final check before we discharge you."

Sean quickly got the hang of walking in paper slippers. Ten minutes later, he'd made it to the end of the corridor outside his room and reached a glassed-in balcony that overlooked downtown Glory. He tried to gauge the damage Gilda had caused. All of the windows he could see were intact, but roof shingles were missing here and there. Soon after Sean maneuvered past the heavy glass door and stepped onto the balcony, a tall, official-looking man introduced himself.

"I'm Rafe Neilson. I'm glad to see you up and about. You looked awfully shaky last night, and they wouldn't let me speak to you."

"What do you want to talk about?"

"The fatal accident at the church."

"The fellow who took care of the church's generator?"

Rafe nodded. "Richard Squires. I sang in the church choir with him. We'd become good friends during the five years I've lived in Glory."

"That's the one thing I hate about hurricanes—they kill

people. No one told me that he was dead, but I guessed as much when I heard Ann Trask shouting."

"I understand that you tried to start the church's generator."

"Ann asked me to."

"Why do you suppose she did that?"

Sean shrugged. "I'd told her that we have a generator in our broadcast van. I guess she assumed I'd know how to work the church's backup system. I showed her where the manual start button was, and things were fine for a few seconds. I gave up as soon as I saw the fuel system warning light blinking red. I had a broadcast coming up and didn't have time to work on the engine. That's when I told Ann to call Richard Squires."

"How did you know about Richard?"

"A note tacked to the wall said to contact him if the generator didn't work." Sean felt a twinge of concern. The surprisingly formal tone of Rafe's questions had put him on edge. "You're beginning to sound like a policeman, Rafe."

"Can't help it," he said with a grin. "I'm Glory's deputy police chief. We don't have many fatal accidents in our little town. I'm trying to understand everything that happened in Glory Community's parking lot last night."

"A gust of wind at the height of the hurricane tore the steeple down—a gust with a velocity of upwards of ninety miles per hour. The wreckage fell on Richard Squires and our broadcast van. What more is there to understand?"

Rafe shook his head. "Probably nothing. Take care of yourself. Don't overdo."

Before Sean could reply, Rafe pivoted on his heels and began to walk away.

"Hey, Mr. Deputy Police Chief. I have a question for you. How badly did Glory get hit last night?"

"Not badly at all," Rafe said over his shoulder. "A handful of large trees are down, a few windows broken here and there, several dozen roofs were damaged, and the streets nearest the Albemarle Sound were flooded, including part of Front Street. We got off lucky except for Richard's death and the fallen steeple. Other than you and your colleague, there were no injuries requiring hospitalization."

Rafe departed, leaving Sean to speculate what had prompted the string of odd questions. He returned to his room and sat down on the visitor's chair in front of his bed. A short time later a nurse's aide arrived with his breakfast tray and placed it on a wheeled table next to the chair.

"I'm not usually a grits person but these look good," Sean said as he grabbed a spoon to dig in.

The door squeaked open and Sharon propelled Carlo, sitting regally in a wheelchair, into the room. Sean noted that Carlo's forehead and left eye were both bandaged, the dressing on his eye smaller than the bandage Sean remembered from the night before.

"Here you go, Mr. Vaughn," she said. "This is your room. Can you manage to climb into bed, or do you need me to help you?"

"I wouldn't dream of saying no to anything you offer, Sharon," Carlo said, punctuating his smarmy reply with an utterly sincere gaze. "Please, please, please call me Carlo."

Sharon seemed to tolerate Carlo's obvious flirtation, although Sean could barely avoid throwing a spoonful of grits at him.

"Good morning, amigo," Sean said. "You look much better than you did last night. What did the doctors tell you?"

Carlo gestured toward his bandaged eye. "This is the

worrisome injury. A glass splinter scratched my cornea and lifted a small flap of tissue. It should heal cleanly—but there's always a risk of infection." He touched his forehead. "I also have a concussion," Carlo said. "Worse than yours, but I'll probably survive. The MRI didn't show any long-term damage."

Sean bit back a snicker. They'd looked inside Carlo's head and found nothing.

"Glad to hear it. So far so good."

"The docs want me to stay in the hospital two or three more days."

"The nursing staff requested a whole week," Sharon said, winking at Sean, "but Carlo's insurance company wouldn't agree to cover more than three days." She helped him climb into bed. "Would you like breakfast?"

"No thanks. My stomach feels too wonky to eat." Carlo's voice oozed angst and made known the enormity of his self-sacrifice. Sharon smiled as she left the room.

Carlo pointed at Sean's tray. "I see that you're able to eat breakfast."

"Eagerly, in fact."

"Good. I'd hate unnecessary guilt to put you off your feed."

"Why would I feel the least bit guilty?"

"You chose the parking place last night, not me."

Sean ate more grits. There was no point arguing with Carlo when he got hold of a loony idea.

Someone knocked on the door.

"Come in," Sean said.

The door opened, revealing Ann Trask. Sean realized that Ann was petite—five foot three and a hundred pounds, at the most. But the strength that radiated from her blue eyes made her seem a foot taller.

"Hello, gentlemen," Ann said.

"It's *Mizz* Ann Trask," Carlo said, "come to visit the halt and the lame. A very churchy thing to do."

It was rare for Carlo to offer a verbal joke, so Sean kept it going. "We're both a tad halt today, Ann, but no more lame than usual."

He expected Ann to react, but she didn't even crack a smile. She probably didn't feel like laughing so soon after Richard Squires's death. But he saw another emotion in her somber expression. Something beyond grief that looked like worry.

Carlo must have also registered Ann's mood. He offered a high-voltage smile and said, "I haven't forgotten my promise to put you on the Storm Channel. What's your schedule like during the next day or two?"

She responded with a small smile of her own. "Let's wait until your bandages are off. If I'm going to debut on television with Carlo Vaughn, I insist on the unadorned original."

"You shall have him, although a black eye patch can be an intriguing fashion accessory. I may adopt the buccaneer look. What do you think?"

Sean felt like retching, but Carlo's cornball patter had amplified Ann's smile and chased the worry—if that's what he had seen—from her face.

"You'd make a great swashbuckling buccaneer," she said, making Sean wish that he had the skill to say magic words that could alter a woman's frame of mind.

Even more to the point, he wished that Ann smiled at him the way she smiled at Carlo.

FOUR

Ann felt the cool breeze play around her head as she walked from the hospital back to Glory Community Church. She felt bad that she hadn't been an especially cheerful visitor, although Carlo had been cheerful enough for everyone. And how could she feel anything but gloomy? Phil Meade's unfair accusations weighed on her. Worse yet, she suspected that Phil held another shoe, and she was waiting for it to drop. Perhaps he'd dug into her past and was prepared to confront her with it.

The more she thought about it, the more she concluded that Rafe had been wrong to tell her to wait before talking to Phil Meade. She should have confronted him immediately the previous night. Phil owed her an apology for disputing her need to call on Richard to fix the generator—and the quicker she told him that, the better. Dealing with Phil was like removing a Band-Aid. Getting it over in one painful yank was much better than a series of throbbing tugs.

She glanced at her watch. A quarter to two. She'd planned to spend the remainder of the afternoon inventorying the damage to the church grounds. She'd also hoped to go see how the little house she shared with her mother had fared during the storm. Both chores left plenty of time for a brief detour to see Phil Meade at the command center. Why not visit him right now?

Ann had never been inside Glory's emergency command center, but she remembered Rafe saying it was part of police headquarters.

She hadn't slept a wink during the height of the storm, and although no one had sought shelter inside the church, she'd made sure that everything was ready for the aftermath. Ann had managed a nap between three and six in the morning. Then she'd spent more than an hour reshelving the cans of food and bottles of water she'd hauled out of the church's pantry the day before. She also returned a dozen still-wrapped camp cots to the basement storeroom and restacked the accompanying blankets.

Two of the church's elders had arrived at eight to evaluate the damage to the building, including Maury Collins, a licensed building inspector. "God watched over us," he'd said. "The storm could have taken down the whole steeple and destroyed the roof, but it didn't. The top three-quarters of the steeple is gone, but the base is still firmly attached to the roof. Most of the church's heavy-duty shingles survived, leaving the interior of the roof dry. The bottom line is that the church building is perfectly safe to use and replacing the steeple will be a straightforward repair job. We'll look like our old selves in a few months."

Ann walked north on Broad Street. She sidestepped a few dozen broken branches strewn along the pavement and walked past several battered garbage cans that must have been propelled by Gilda's peak winds. The sidewalks were littered with random pieces of wood wrenched from homes and buildings, dozens of unlucky roof shingles, and numerous slabs of torn-away siding.

Ann gazed east on Main Street as she walked through the intersection and saw three large trees toppled on their sides. One had smashed the front window of a fancy boutique. The street sign at the corner of Main and Broad had been bent in half like a paper clip, a testimony to the power of a hurricane. She reminded herself that Glory had escaped the worst of Gilda's winds. What would the town look like this afternoon if the hurricane had made a direct hit? she wondered. It was awful to even think about.

The few vehicles on the street were trucks driven by repair personnel. The citizenry of Glory had wisely followed the police department's advice to keep the streets clear of cars. The traffic lights were cycling green, yellow and red, which meant that the electricity had been restored to downtown. Ann heard the whine of power saws in the distance—a surprisingly reassuring noise signaling another step in the journey to restore normalcy to Glory.

Ann crossed to the western side of Broad Street and walked past Glory Baptist Church. Gilda had shattered the church's illuminated sign, throwing plastic letters across the front lawn and driveway. The only intact part of the sign was the pastor's name at the top. The sight of it made Ann wish that the pastor of Glory Community Church, Daniel Hartman, was home. He was a good listener, always supportive, and chock-full of practical wisdom. The very sort of person she needed to talk to right now.

Well, don't expect to have your hand held for another day or two. Daniel is rushing home from his honeymoon so that he can comfort people who've suffered serious loss, not people who can't seem to get along.

Daniel and Lori were scheduled to arrive in Norfolk at dinnertime, but they would still have the challenge of driving to Glory. Several of the roads from the airport had been directly under the storm, and they might be flooded out or closed by debris. But Ann knew Daniel—news of a dead choir member and a smashed steeple would encourage him to press on no matter what. *Please, God, don't let him take foolish risks.*

She made a mental note: Open up and air out the church's manse on Oliver Street. And if the supermarket on King Street is open, pick up eggs, milk, bread and a few other staples for the Hartman's refrigerator.

Ann turned left on Campbell Street. Without thinking, she looked to the right, expecting to see the tip of Glory Community's steeple in the distance, over the rooftops.

With God's help, she thought, everything would soon be back to normal. *But can we rely on God's help? He's been spotty when it comes to helping me.*

A few more steps brought Ann to the front of Glory's redbrick police headquarters. The building was alive with people coming and going. A sign outside told her the emergency command center in the back had its own entrance. She followed the paved path to a utilitarian cinder-block structure. She hesitated, then pushed the intercom button.

"Ann Trask to see Phil Meade."

Moments later, the door swung open. Phil had come to get her. Without greeting her, he stepped backward from the door and waved her in.

Ann followed him into a large, brightly lit room full of computer monitors. The screens were blank; the command center didn't seem to be commanding anything.

"We're getting ready to shut down the command center," Phil said, as if reading her mind. "Another ten minutes and you would have missed me. I'd have gone back to my day job."

Ann nodded. She knew that Phil ran a successful consulting business helping small cities enhance their emergency preparedness.

He continued, "What can I do for you?"

"We need to talk," Ann said.

He led her to an especially large desk in the back of the room. "Okay. Let's talk."

Ann hoped her expression communicated geniality. "Let me begin by saying that you upset me last night. There's no way that I can defend myself against that kind of attack. All I can say is that Richard Squires was my friend, too. I certainly didn't intend to put him in harm's way. Neither did I mean to shift any blame to Richard—I know he worked hard to keep the generator running. I spoke in anger last night, and that was wrong of me. Please forgive me."

He gestured toward a chair next to his desk. "I should have offered you a seat when you came in. I seem to have forgotten my manners, and for that I apologize. Let's both sit down."

"Thank you." She dropped into the seat, watching Phil's face as he settled into the swivel chair behind his desk. He seemed much less belligerent than the night before. Perhaps the worst was over?

He made a small grimace and said, "I also want to apologize if anything I said suggested that you purposely hurt Richard Squires. I know that isn't true."

She offered a tentative smile to signal her acceptance of his apology.

"But," Phil went on, "I completely reject your argument that a quirk of fate put Richard in the church parking lot at the exact instant that the steeple came tumbling down. He was there for one reason—you called him."

Ann tried to read the expression on Phil's face but couldn't decipher his mood. Nonetheless, despite his harsh words, she and Phil seemed to be engaged in a civil conversation, with each participant listening patiently to the other. So far, so good.

"I've thought long and hard about last night, and I feel certain about one thing," Ann said. "If I could do it all over again, I would still call Richard. My decision to ask him for help was the right thing to do. In the hours before Gilda struck Glory, everyone I spoke to anticipated a disaster, saying that the power would fail within hours. For that reason, it was absolutely necessary that our backup generator work reliably. It would be our sole source of lighting and ventilation. Without it, the church couldn't have accommodated anyone seeking refuge from the storm. Last night, you accused me of being afraid of the dark. To some extent, you're right. I was afraid that a dark and powerless church would be a useless emergency shelter."

Phil frowned deeply. Ann thought about stopping but decided to keep going. She might as well say all that she'd come to say. "As you know, the power in Glory was off all night. In fact, it was still off early this morning when I left the church. But our backup generator worked perfectly all night, thanks to Richard."

"Are you finished?" Phil asked. "Or do you have additional self-serving claptrap to present to me?" He held up both hands, his palms facing Ann. "Please go without saying anything more. I don't enjoy proving that you are a liar."

"Nothing I've said to you has been a lie," Ann said, trying to keep the anger out of her voice.

"Oh, but it has, Ann. The worst kind of lie—a lie to yourself." Phil stood and perched on the edge of his desk, leaning toward her. "All of us concerned with public safety occasionally make poor decisions. That goes with the territory, because emergency situations force us to stick our necks out.

"I wouldn't fault you if you'd made a simple mistake last night. But that's not what happened. You didn't arrive at a thoughtful decision to bring Richard to the church for the benefit of people who might have to stay in the shelter. You called him because you were frightened."

Ann wanted to argue, but the curiously confident look on Phil's face made her hesitate.

"I want you to hear something," Phil said. He lifted a compact tape recorder from a drawer and placed it on his desk. "We record all of the telephone calls coming in to the emergency command center."

Ann felt her heart patter wildly. She tried to remember what she had said to Richard, but couldn't summon up her exact words or recall her tone of voice. Had she sounded apprehensive? It was possible. She'd definitely been worried.

He pressed Play.

Her voice emerged from the machine's speaker. "Richard, it's Ann Trask, at the church. I tried to start the generator. It ran for a few seconds, then died. Something's wrong with the fuel system. I don't want to spend the night inside a pitch-black church during a hurricane if the power fails. The note on the wall says to call you in case of trouble. Can you come over right away?"

Phil Meade rose to his feet. "Do you want me to play it again? I want to make certain that you heard the frightened tremor in your voice."

"There's no need to play it again, Phil," Ann said, struggling to conceal her embarrassment.

"I didn't think you'd want me to. There's not a hint in your call to Richard that you were concerned about the emergency shelter. The call is all about you being alone in the church in the dark. You dragged Richard out unnecessarily and put him in danger. That's why he ended up in the parking lot during the height of the storm. Had you waited for a true emergency—or for the heavy winds to abate—he would have escaped the falling steeple."

Ann tried to find a good way to challenge Phil's conclusion, but the recording had shaken her. Anyone who listened to the tape would agree with Phil. She could try to explain everything that was going on in her mind when she made the call, but Phil would only use it against her to make his point: that she shouldn't have been left in charge of the emergency shelter.

Phil's expression had grown dark and foreboding. He wagged a menacing finger at her and his voice rose. "I intend to make certain that you never again hold a position of responsibility in Glory that might put people's lives at risk."

She suddenly realized that Phil's voice had carried throughout the room. She glanced around and found that the other people in the command center were staring at her. Glaring, actually. Except for Rafe Neilson, who seemed distressed by Phil's tirade.

"We obviously have nothing more to talk about," she said to Phil, amazed at the false bravado she'd been able to sustain in her own voice.

Then she stood up and walked slowly toward the door, determined to maintain her dignity. Once outside, another voice assailed her as she ran down the path that led to Campbell Street—one from deep inside her own mind. *Rafe was right, after all. You did make things worse by confronting Phil Meade.*

She strode west toward King Street and wondered what Phil meant by his nasty threat.

He can't be serious. He's merely blowing off steam. But in her heart of hearts, Ann knew that wasn't true. Phil Meade had become an unwavering adversary.

On Wednesday morning, Sean tried to convince the hospital that he was well enough to walk but Sharon R.N. had insisted on calling a taxi. When Sean stepped out of a Glorious Cab in front of the Scottish Captain after a ridiculous two-block ride up Broad Street, the cabdriver echoed Sharon's recommendation. "You'll love The Captain. Emma Neilson operates one of the best B and Bs in North Carolina."

Sean pressed the button next to the front door and heard a chime ring somewhere deep inside the pretty three-story white clapboard building. The door swung open and Sean found himself face-to-face with Deputy Police Chief Rafe Neilson.

The penny dropped. Emma Neilson. Rafe Neilson. *Same last name.*

"Rafe, I need a place to stay until our broadcast van is livable and drivable again."

Rafe smiled at him. "I can accommodate you at the jail but my wife's in charge of rooms at the Scottish Captain. Make yourself at home in the parlor—I'll tell her you're here."

Sean settled himself into a deeply padded chaise lounge near the parlor door. He heard Rafe's footsteps retreat to the back of the house, and he promptly dozed off.

"Mr. Miller?"

Sean awoke with a start to find an attractive woman standing over him. She was in her mid-thirties, with short dark hair and big brown eyes.

"My apologies for waking you," she said. "That chaise is more soporific than a sleeping pill." She held out her hand. "I'm Emma."

Sean leveraged himself to his feet. "I need a room for a few days. I won't know exactly how long until I commission a repair shop to fix our broadcast van."

"We have six rooms—you can take your pick." Emma gave a sardonic chuckle. "Gilda chased away our guests this week. Do you need help with your luggage?"

Sean shook his head. "My stuff is still inside the Storm Channel broadcast van. I'll retrieve it this afternoon."

"Have you had lunch yet?"

"That's another item on my to-do list."

"Rafe and I were sampling an experimental quiche whipped up by my breakfast chef, Calvin Constable. He's known for his oddball combinations. Why don't you help us decide if this one works?"

"Well, I do feel a bit peckish. Breakfast at the hospital didn't exactly satisfy."

"Follow me." Emma led Sean into the Captain's kitchen to a large round table and seated him opposite Rafe. She poured a cup of coffee and put a slice of quiche in front of him. "This should alleviate your peckishness."

Sean used a fork to break off a chunk. He needed several seconds to identify the mystery quiche's chief ingredients: Gorgonzola cheese, tomatoes, pepperoni, asparagus, anchovies and zucchini.

"I want your honest opinion," Emma said.

"I've already given you mine," Rafe said. "The first word that springs to mind is 'yuck.' Calvin is a great cook but a rotten inventor. This crazy mishmash tastes like pizza-flavored cat food." Rafe took a swig of coffee and began to gargle with it. He swallowed abruptly when

Emma poked him in the stomach. "I'd arrest the man if it wasn't so difficult to find a good breakfast chef."

"I'd still like to know what Sean thinks," Emma said.

Rafe laughed as he stood up and walked toward a window. "The proof of the pudding is in the eating—and Sean has stopped eating."

Sean debated his answer and finally decided that Emma needed nothing but the truth. "I have to agree with Rafe. 'Yuck' is an apt description for this particular quiche."

"A customer has spoken," Rafe said. "A hungry customer, to boot. Serve him one of Calvin's sausage pies," Rafe said. "They're delectable." He opened the back door. "Hey! I just saw the paperboy ride down Broad Street on his bike. Maybe we'll have a newspaper today, after all."

Sean had just lifted a forkful of sausage pie to his mouth when Rafe reappeared and said, "Talk about bad taste. This is a new low."

"I take it you're no longer talking about Calvin's quiche," Emma said.

"Rex Grainger published a special six-page hurricane edition of the *Glory Gazette*. Wait until you see the photograph he put at the top of page one." Rafe dropped the abbreviated newspaper on the kitchen table.

Sean caught a glimpse of the front page and forgot the few uneaten bites of sausage pie. "That's the fallen steeple," he said, "and what's left of the Storm Channel's broadcast van."

"Oh my goodness!" Emma poked at the photo with her index finger. "Am I seeing what I think I'm seeing?"

"'Fraid so," Rafe said. "Those are Richard's boots. The rest of him is covered by rubble."

"I remember that sight," Sean said, "but I don't remember any photographers taking pictures."

"Check the credit," Emma said. "Rex Grainger shot the picture himself."

"Phil Meade is going to skin him alive," Rafe said.

"Well, at least he can't blame Ann for the photo," Emma said.

"I'm not so sure," Rafe said. "He's blamed her for everything else."

"Who is Phil Meade?" Sean asked Emma.

Sean noted the cease-and-desist look that Rafe cast at Emma. She ignored it and answered Sean's asked—and unasked—questions.

"Phil is Glory's director of emergency management. He blames Ann for Richard's death."

"Why?"

"Because she called Richard to the church."

"Then he should also blame me," Sean said. "I told Ann to call Richard to fix the generator."

"Maybe you should explain that to Phil," Emma said.

Rafe brought his hands together in the T-shaped timeout signal known to all football fans. "Bad idea! The more people who talk to Phil, the angrier he gets at Ann. Leave Phil alone—he needs time to cool off. He'll figure out all by himself that he's wrong."

"No he won't," Emma said.

"Why doesn't anybody ever listen to me?" Rafe asked.

"Look at this," Sean said. "It's Ann's garage."

The photo showed a tree limb poking through the roof of a detached garage behind a house. The caption read *Gilda visited the Trask residence on Queen Street and proved to be an unwelcome guest.*

Sean made out the number above the front door: 110.

"She didn't mention the damage this morning."

"I'm not sure she knows about it yet," Rafe said. "I think she spent the night at the church."

"When did you meet Ann?" Emma asked Sean.

"Yesterday. Last night, she rescued me from the storm. This morning, she visited Carlo and me in the hospital."

"She's a lovely woman," Emma said. "Caring, smart as a whip, charming—and single, too."

Rafe smiled at Sean. "In case you haven't figured it out yet, my wife is a dyed-in-the-wool amateur matchmaker."

When Sean finished eating, he walked the few blocks to Glory Community Church. He surveyed the destruction to the broadcast van and rescued his duffel full of clothing from the hanging locker. His belongings had survived the storm along with most of the van's electronic equipment.

He called Cathy at the Storm Channel's broadcast headquarters on his cell. "I estimate that Carlo will probably be fixed quicker than the van. It needs a radiator, a windshield, headlights, some interior fixes and lots of front-end bodywork. I'll have some temporary repairs made so I can drive the van north."

"How's your head?" she asked.

"No better or worse than before."

She chuckled. "In that case, we'll leave you in Glory to watch over the van and Carlo. Keep me informed of their conditions."

Sean closed his cell and asked a man working on trees for directions to Oliver Street. He had no difficulty finding Ann's house. The big tree limb stabbing through the roof of her detached garage was visible from the street. The smaller branches had lost most of their leaves, making the limb look like some kind of bizarre TV antenna. Gilda had also ravaged most of the plants in Ann's garden. A miniature forest of broken stems served as a reminder of what had been lost.

Ann was sitting on her front steps, her arms wrapped around herself. She looked utterly miserable—yet surprisingly pretty despite her obvious gloom.

"Sean," she said when she spotted him. "You've come to visit me."

Sean wanted to find the perfect words that would offer her comfort. But all he could manage was, "I'm so sorry about your garage, Ann." He dug in his pocket and came up with an unused tissue for her.

"Thanks," she said, accepting the tissue and quickly wiping away a tear.

He sat down next to her. "I know you have a plateful of other problems today."

"What do you mean?" she asked, alarmed.

"I heard about the nasty things Glory's emergency management director said to you."

"How do you know about my meeting with Phil Meade?" Her eyes flashed angrily as she stared at him.

"I saw Rafe Neilson this morning." Ann stood up and began to pace the porch. "You shouldn't be taking heat for calling Richard Squires to the church. After all, I suggested—"

"Talk about rotten!" Ann said. "If you've heard what Phil said to me, then most of Glory probably knows about it by now."

"Phil sounds like a stupid blowhard."

Ann's response was not what he expected. "Please don't take my side in a battle you don't understand," she said. "You've never met Phil Meade. More important, you don't know anything about me."

Before he could reply, she went inside her house and closed the door without uttering another word.

Sean wondered what had gone wrong. Something he'd said had prompted Ann's mysterious reaction. But for the life of him he couldn't fathom what kind of verbal gaffe he'd committed. All he'd wanted to do was defend her.

One thing's for sure, Miller. You have a magic touch with the ladies.

FIVE

Ann watched through the peephole in her front door. She felt an unexpected ache of sadness as Sean headed down her walk toward the street. Why had she cut him off so rudely? An answer popped into her mind: *You like Sean Miller more than you're willing to acknowledge.*

"Don't be silly," she murmured. Her cell phone rang, interrupting her thoughts. She looked at her phone and saw "Church Manse." Daniel Hartman was calling her from his home.

"Daniel! You're back in Glory!"

"Lori and I spent last night in Norfolk," he said. "We drove home first thing this morning."

"I can't tell you how happy I am to know that you're only two blocks away from me."

Ann felt a wave of relief wash over her. With her mother across the state, there'd been no one she could talk to, nowhere to go for advice. She knew that Daniel would listen to her tale of woe and help her find a way through the maze of difficulties.

"I'm happy to be home," Daniel said.

"The senior pastor of Glory Community Church

shouldn't tell industrial-strength untruths. Everyone knows that Gilda ruined your honeymoon."

"Cut short by a few days, perhaps, but definitely not ruined. Lori and I had a glorious time. Besides, we plan to spend the next several days shopping in Glory. It'll be just like a honeymoon!"

"Shopping?"

"Lori starts her new job as one of Glory's Finest in less than two weeks. She has a long list of items to buy before then, including stuff for the manse, police equipment, and dozens of personal purchases. I promised not to complain if—I mean *when*—she goes over budget."

"Well, welcome back, Daniel. I won't take any more of your precious time today," she said.

"Not so fast. You're forgetting that I called you."

"No, I'm not. But you must be tired from all the traveling you did yesterday. And I'm sure that your new wife would like to spend a little quiet time with you."

"It was my new wife who told me to call you, and ordered me to make sure that I talk to you about the damage to your house as well as your set-to with Phil Meade and the outrageous things he said to you."

"You've heard about that."

"Glory is a tight-knit little community. Sooner or later, local pastors hear about most things. In this case, it was sooner."

"From a little birdie named Rafe Neilson," Ann said.

"I'd rather not name names, but it wasn't Rafe who brought me up-to-date."

Ann felt an icy shiver creep along her spine. Daniel's birdie must have been Phil Meade himself. Talking to Daniel was step one in fulfilling the threat that Phil had made to her.

Daniel reacted to her silence. "Ann, who cares about

talkative birds? All that matters right now is you. Where are you?"

"In my kitchen. With empty ice-cream containers."

"It's the middle of the morning."

"True. But I was up most of last night, thinking about Richard Squires and Phil Meade."

"Do you have any ice cream left?"

"I finished the last of the chocolate about an hour ago."

"Persevere! I'll be there in ten minutes with additional supplies," Daniel said.

"You're coming here?"

"Unless you tell me you won't open the door."

She laughed. "Bring Rocky Road. And thank Lori as you leave."

Ann felt a weight being lifted from her shoulders. Perhaps Daniel—a formidable ally—was on her side. And perhaps Phil would see the situation differently if Daniel was helping to make her case.

The cavalry has arrived, she thought. Well, not quite. Daniel didn't ride a horse, but he had spent more than twenty years as a U.S. Army chaplain. He qualified as cavalry.

Ann opened the front door when she heard Daniel's car in her driveway. He greeted her with a hug and an insulated paper bag. "I hope a half gallon is enough."

"Barely," she said, with as broad a grin as she could muster. She took a step backward so that she could look at him. He seemed relaxed and happy. No surprise there— he was a newlywed who'd just returned from his honeymoon.

"Follow me to the kitchen table. There's work to be done." She slipped the carton of ice cream out of the bag, serving them each double scoops of Rocky Road in dessert bowls.

Daniel rested his elbows on the table. "You took on a huge responsibility on Monday night, Ann. The elders are grateful for your courageous decision to remain on duty inside the church."

She shook her head. "They won't feel that way after Phil Meade talks to them. He blames me for Richard Squires's death."

"Well, he blames you for calling Richard to the church unnecessarily, as he puts it."

"Did another birdie tell you that?" Ann asked, trying to smile.

"You have a right to know that that came directly from the horse's mouth."

"Did Phil also tell you that he chewed me out yesterday?"

Daniel nodded. "Proudly. Although he admitted that you are a tough nut to crack."

For a brief moment, Ann wondered if Phil would be able to change Daniel's mind about her. After all, Phil was a dynamic and impressive person, a force to be reckoned with in Glory. She quickly dismissed the notion. Daniel wasn't the sort of man who wavered. He stood solidly in her corner.

Praise the Lord for that.

A new worry tore through her mind and generated an even sharper chill. Would Daniel remain supportive if he learned her whole story? The information about her past was out there—anyone who entered her name in an Internet search engine would learn most of her history in a few seconds. Two or three phone calls would fill in the rest. Maybe now was a good time to tell Daniel what had happened seven years ago.

No. He doesn't need more to worry about right now.

She ate a spoonful of ice cream and then asked, "Do you think I called Richard to the church unnecessarily?"

"The only person who can answer that question is you."

"But that doesn't stop people from speculating and telling me what they think."

"Ah. You've had phone calls?"

"Two. One woman said I was an inspiration to every female in Glory because I had the courage to stay in town during the storm. Another woman told me I was stupid and that Richard Squires would still be alive if someone who knew how to fix generators had been in charge of the emergency shelter."

"Oh, dear. Did you recognize their voices?"

"'Fraid not. Does it matter?"

"Not unless they're members of the church. Taking sides in a situation like this can drive a wedge through a congregation. The first chance I get, I'll point out to our members that the church steeple, which was built nearly ninety years ago, survived several other strong storms. No one but God could know that Gilda would blow it into the parking lot. And that includes Ann Trask, intrepid church administrator."

"Thank you, Daniel."

He added, "People also need to be reminded that Richard put himself in charge of our emergency generator. He'd have been furious if you hadn't called him to repair it."

"That's what I thought, too." Ann sighed. "But Phil insists that Richard came out during the storm only because of me, and that he didn't want to leave the command center."

Daniel reached across the table and placed his hand over hers. He'd obviously heard this part of the story, too. "Can't you guess why Rafe didn't argue with Phil when he said that?"

"I haven't a clue."

"Rafe knew that Phil was upset. He didn't want to fight with him minutes after Richard's body had been taken away."

Ann smiled. "I know the name Daniel means 'the Lord is my judge.' But you're not the least bit judgmental. I should start calling you Peter, because you're my rock. I feel better now—and that's not just the ice cream talking. Thank you."

"On that note, I feel a prayer coming on."

Ann closed her eyes and bowed her head.

"Heavenly Father," Daniel began, "I thank You this glorious Wednesday morning—a reminder that all storms eventually come to an end. I thank You also for sending Ann Trask to Glory Community Church. I ask You to comfort Ann, to sustain her, and to equip her to serve You. Give her the wisdom to do what is right in Your eyes, and the strength to look beyond unfair criticisms offered by confused but well-intentioned people. I ask these things in Jesus' name. Amen."

Daniel and Ann stood up from the table, and he pulled her into a hug. "I'd better go see how much money Lori's spent in my absence. By the way, when Lori and I got home, we were delighted to find the manse ready for our return. I'm astonished that you thought about us with so much going on. God bless you, Ann."

Ann decided to stay put in the kitchen. If she walked Daniel to the door, she might start crying, which would embarrass both of them.

"Give my love to Lori," she managed to say without her voice cracking.

"I hope I'm not making another mistake," Sean muttered as he climbed the steps to Ann Trask's front porch. He'd arrived just as a tall, distinguished-looking man with a thick head of reddish brown hair had left the house and driven away.

"Who could that have been?" he asked himself, feeling an unpleasant twinge of jealousy.

How can I be jealous of other men? Ann wants nothing to do with me.

He murmured the Doxology to buttress his courage and knocked softly on the front door.

"I'll be right there." Ann spoke from somewhere deep inside the house.

"Take your time," Sean said, before he could stop himself. *Sheesh! That sounded stupid.*

The door opened.

"Sean Miller!" Ann exclaimed.

"Ann Trask!" he mimicked. "I hope you don't mind me showing up unannounced for the second time this morning. I was in the neighborhood and decided to drop by."

"I don't mind. I promise I'll do my best not to slam the door in your face this time."

"I figure that was mostly my fault. You didn't need an unexpected visitor, what with all you went through yesterday and a tree poking through the roof of your garage."

She joined him on the porch and gestured toward two side-by-side Adirondack chairs. Sean sat in one; Ann took the other. He risked a direct look at her face. She seemed in a good mood, and not especially upset to see him.

"I talked with my brother about the tree," she said. "He checked with our insurance company, and we're covered for wind damage. He arranged to have a contractor repair the roof."

As she talked, her fingers played with a bright blue almond-shaped object that dangled from a lanyard around her neck. Sean wondered if it performed a function or was merely decorative.

"That's splendid news," Sean said, smiling at her and—hooray!—she smiled back. A pretty smile that lit up her face.

Stop staring at her. She'll think you're a dunce.

"So, Sean, what brought you to Queen Street?"

"I had to meet with Tucker Mackenzie at the Glory Garage. It seems the steeple did more damage to our broadcast van than anyone realized at first."

"When will you leave Glory?" she asked.

"Friday at the earliest. When the van is roadworthy, I'll drive it back to Long Island. Carlo may also be ready for a new assignment by then. He'll fly home."

She nodded. " 'Storms come, storms go. We follow the storms.' "

"I hate that harebrained slogan. I want to predict storms, not follow them," Sean said.

"It must be interesting to spend so much time on the move."

"The truth is it gets stale quickly. I look forward to living a settled life after I finish paying for my education."

Stop the small talk. Get to the point.

"Ann, I had to deal with the Glory Garage, but I also wanted to talk to you about something that's been on my mind since yesterday. It kept me wide awake most of the night."

"There's a lot of that going around. What's up?"

"I had a weird thought about the night that Gilda arrived in Glory."

"How weird?"

"Weird enough to ask that you don't say I'm crazy until after I finish explaining my notion," Sean said.

She shrugged. "This is my weird morning. I've eaten enough chocolate ice cream to cater a kid's birthday party and it's not even noon. I'm not sure you can tell me anything more bizarre than that."

"Wanna bet? Okay, I'll spit it out. I don't think Richard Squires's death was an accident. In fact, I'm sure that it wasn't. The falling steeple didn't kill him."

"Not an accident? What are you suggesting?" She caught her breath. "If the falling steeple didn't kill Richard—"

He finished the sentence she'd begun. "Something else killed him. More likely, *someone* else did."

"But that's…that's *murder*."

"Cold-blooded murder."

"I won't say you're crazy, Sean, but lack of sleep has clearly muddled your brain. Everyone in Glory loved Richard Squires. Why would anyone murder him?"

"I went to the library this morning and browsed through a textbook on criminal investigation. Detectives look for three things when they try to solve a murder—motive, means and opportunity. When it comes to Richard Squires, I'm still hazy about motive, but I've begun to zero in on means and opportunity."

"I take it back," Ann said. "You are crazy."

"Give me another minute, and I'll prove to you I'm not."

Ann didn't say anything, which Sean took as an invitation to carry on.

"Three things about Richard's death are suspicious and suggest that he wasn't the victim of a freak accident. First, Richard finished working on the generator at the point of highest wind and greatest rainfall. But he didn't walk directly from the church to his car. For some reason, he took a detour past our broadcast van. That makes no sense at all."

Ann pictured the church's parking lot during Gilda. Sean was right. Richard's car was parked in the rear of the lot and the van in the middle, much closer to the church's side door. Why would Richard detour past the van during a hurricane?

"Richard liked technology," Ann suggested. "Perhaps he wanted to check out your van and the satellite antenna on the roof."

"Possibly, but what kind of view could he have had? The rain would have pummeled his face if he looked up."

"Good point," Ann admitted. "What's the second suspicious thing?"

"The falling wreckage would have hit Richard from behind. There's no way he could have landed on his back, stretched out, face up, with his boots pointing at the sky." Sean reached into his jacket pocket. "Here's yesterday's *Glory Gazette.* You saw the scene for real before the photographer took this picture."

Ann turned away. Sean understood her reluctance. She didn't need to see a photograph of Richard Squires under the fallen steeple. The grim image was undoubtedly etched in her mind.

Sean put the paper away and continued. "Richard should have fallen forward in a heap or crumpled to one side. Think about it."

"I don't know enough about falling wreckage to decide one way or the other."

"Well, I do know. I've studied the aftermaths of dozens of hurricanes. The victims don't look like someone went to the trouble of arranging their bodies neatly under piles of broken boards."

"Okay, what's the third suspicious thing?" she asked.

"I'm sorry to bring this up, but if a falling steeple the size of a small house had actually hit Richard, there would have been lots more damage to his face and head. I woke up inside the ambulance. The interior lights were on and I saw Richard's face. I noticed a few scratches, but no significant injuries."

He watched Ann shudder. "I get the idea," she said, taking several calming breaths.

"Let's move on to the bottom line. Someone in Glory wanted Richard Squires dead, and that same someone used Gilda as a cover for murder. All of which means that your telephone call had absolutely nothing to do with Richard's death. He would have died even if the generator had kept running when we started it."

Ann pursed her lips. "Sean, I appreciate what you're trying to do, but your theory—if that's what it is—has a zillion flaws. I've never read a criminal investigation textbook, but my mother and I love to read murder mysteries." She began to count on her fingers.

"First, Richard was an all-around nice guy. He'd lived in Glory forever and had a million friends and no enemies. I can't think of a single person who'd want him dead. You'll never find a motive to kill Richard, because there isn't one.

"Second, this is a quiet little town. I can't imagine anyone in Glory being devious enough to use a hurricane to camouflage a murder.

"Third, Glory had been evacuated. There were only a handful of people left in town that evening—police officers, firefighters, medical personnel and the folks manning the emergency command center. Are you suggesting that one of them killed Richard?"

Sean started to answer her but Ann kept going.

"Fourth, there's probably a simple explanation for the route Richard took through the parking lot. Maybe he became disoriented by the dark, the wind and the rain.

"Fifth, Rafe Neilson and his colleagues aren't stupid. They saw Richard's body. If there were something wrong with its location or the amount of damage, Rafe would have spotted the inconsistencies.

"Sixth…" She hesitated, then frowned. "Your idea is wacky from top to bottom." Ann drew her arms around herself. "No one in Glory will believe that someone murdered Richard Squires. Starting with me."

"Then perhaps I should share my idea with Rafe Neilson, and possibly even Phil Meade?"

Her smile returned. "Rafe will listen politely and then ignore you, but Phil Meade will almost certainly turn the air blue telling you what he thinks of your supposition." Ann suddenly looked at her watch. "I've got to go, Sean. I want to get to the hospital to visit Carlo."

"You're going to see Carlo?" Sean hoped his voice didn't sound as goofy to her as it did to him.

"He's been so nice to me that I thought I'd visit him again. He's all alone in a strange town and he's hurt. It must be awful to lie in a hospital bed with no one to talk to," Ann said.

Sean forced himself to nod noncommittally. The way Ann had announced her plans made it clear that she was looking forward to seeing the Storm Channel's lead weather reporter.

Perhaps he should tell her the truth about Carlo.

He's a louse. You should have heard him talk about you the other evening. Moreover, he's anything but alone in the hospital. By now, Carlo has probably propositioned half the nurses on his floor.

Sean swallowed a sigh.

Leave quietly. She's smitten and won't believe you.

"Well, I'd best be off," he said. "I have another errand to run this morning."

"Thanks for dropping by. I'm sure I'll see you again before you head north."

"You definitely will," Sean said. He walked down the front steps and headed south on Queen Street, without looking back.

Fortunately, she hadn't asked about his errand. He'd decided to sound out Rafe Neilson after all. Ann had judged Carlo Vaughn incorrectly, so perhaps her opinions of Glory's deputy police chief were equally off base.

The three-block walk took Sean less than seven minutes, but as he approached police headquarters, he spotted Rafe driving a police cruiser west. *So much for sounding out the deputy chief.*

Sean was about to head for the Scottish Captain when he had a fresh thought.

Okay, Phil. This seems to be the day when you and I get to meet.

Sean tracked down the telephone number of Glory's emergency command center. A recorded message announced that the center was closed, explaining that Phil Meade could be reached at Meade Consultancy at 350 Main Street.

Ta-da! The joys of a small town.

Sean walked to the brick-faced two-story building and spoke to a bewildered receptionist, who had difficulty dealing with the concept that Sean didn't have an appointment to see Mr. Meade. She finally agreed to call him, and soon thereafter ushered Sean into a large situation room.

Sean immediately identified the top dog. A large man

whose posture declared that he owned the place stood beside a floor-to-ceiling map of North Carolina that covered the rear wall. He held a sandwich in one hand, a coffee mug in the other.

"Mr. Meade," Sean said. "I'm Sean Miller."

"You're one of the Storm Channel folks who were injured the other night."

"That's me."

"What's keeping you in Glory?"

"I can't leave until our weather reporter can travel and our broadcast van is back on the road," Sean explained.

Phil nodded. "Well, Glory has lots to keep you occupied. I urge you to take advantage of our many well-known attractions while you have the opportunity." He finished eating his sandwich and tossed the crumpled wrapper into a waste-paper basket.

"Funny you should say that. I've been keeping myself busy by thinking about the accident the other night, if that's what it really was."

Phil's expression hardened. "If you have something to say to me, young man, say it quickly. Our command center is closed, but there's still emergency work to be done."

"I want to talk to you about Richard Squires's death."

Phil's eyes seemed to bore through him. "Did you know Mr. Squires?"

Sean shook his head. "We never actually met. But I was a few feet away when he died."

"Then what's to talk about?"

"I don't think his death was an accident. See if you agree with me—"

"A church steeple fell on Richard during a hurricane!" Phil interrupted. "How can that be anything but an accident?"

"Just hear me out," Sean said, and quickly reiterated the three observations he'd made to Ann.

Phil's eyes narrowed as he thrust his face close to Sean's. Sean could smell the sandwich on his breath.

"Why, that's about as crazy a theory as I've ever heard. Did Ann Trask send you here to feed me that hogwash?"

"Ann agrees with you. She can't imagine that anyone would want to murder Richard Squires."

"Murder? Who said anything about murder?"

"Well, if Richard didn't die by accident, he was murdered."

Phil's face exploded in anger and Sean took a step back. "Get out of here, Miller!" Phil bellowed. "Now! And if you're wise, you'll get out of Glory before we meet again!"

The handful of other people in the room seemed used to Phil Meade's outbursts. Some offered embarrassed shrugs in response to their boss's behavior. Others glared at Sean, clearly siding with Phil.

"Have a nice day, Mr. Meade," Sean said.

Phil's reply was an obscene gesture. Sean realized that he'd made a new enemy, an unyielding opponent who would never put today's confrontation behind him.

Poor Ann. She shouldn't have to deal with Phil Meade by herself.

"She won't" Sean muttered, as he pushed open the exit door. "Not while I'm in Glory." But before he could help Ann, he would have to convince her to *accept* his help.

That won't be an easy job. She's as stubborn as...well, as I am.

SIX

What could she buy a man who undoubtedly had everything? Ann mused as she strolled past the boutiques on Main Street. The trendiest stores hadn't reopened after Gilda's visit to Glory, but the most touristy of the bunch—the shops that sold tacky souvenirs and T-shirts—were ready for business.

"Fancy meeting you here."

She turned and found Sean Miller grinning at her. A strand of his dark hair had fallen across his forehead. He swiped it away.

"How's Carlo?" he asked.

"I haven't seen him yet. I called my mother after you left, and we spoke longer than I'd meant to. I'm going to the hospital right now. I thought I'd get Carlo a small get-well gift on the way. I've been pondering what to buy without much luck."

"Carlo Vaughn is supremely simple to shop for," Sean said. "He's easily satisfied with the best of everything—or at least, the most expensive."

She cast a sideways glance at Sean. He had tried to come across as flippant, but his lips had drawn into a thin line that signaled deep-seated displeasure with his colleague.

"You don't like Carlo very much, do you?" she said.

"Liking Carlo is not part of my job description." He shrugged. "The truth is, Carlo can be a tough man to work with—or like. He's supremely self-centered, overcritical and difficult to please. I'm enjoying this time away from him."

Ann decided that Sean had a rip-roaring case of Carlo envy. But being judgmental about someone wasn't in *her* job description.

"What about you?" she asked. "Where are you headed?"

"Back to the Scottish Captain. However, I suppose I should take advantage of our fortuitous meeting and fess up." His expression became sheepish. "I ignored your advice and went to see Phil Meade."

"Oh, no!"

"I'll say. You were right about him. He threw me out of his building after I explained my ideas. He also encouraged me to leave Glory."

"Yeow!" Ann exclaimed.

"Well said. He not only didn't buy my conclusions—he assumed that you'd put me up to telling him." Sean grimaced. "I'm sorry if I got you into more trouble with him."

"Regrettably, that's impossible. He hates everything about me. Don't worry about it. You can make it up to me by helping me with a gift for Carlo. Does he like chocolate?"

"Do the citizens of Glory have Southern accents?" He raised a hand to stop her. "You know, I did see something in one of the shops that Carlo might actually like."

"Which one?"

"Follow me."

Ann followed Sean across Main Street. He led her to

the Glorious Giftery and pointed to a display of T-shirts hanging in the front window. The collection included many variations on one theme: I survived Gilda's visit to Glory.

"I'd die before I'd wear those words," Ann said. "Do you really think Carlo would like a grim T-shirt like that?"

"He'd love it. It will become his favorite casual shirt."

"You're not just saying that because you dislike him?" Ann asked.

"Not at all. I think Carlo's a jerk, but leading you astray would make me an even bigger jerk." His grin deepened. "Tell you what. To prove that I'm not pulling your leg, I'll buy one for myself."

Sean held the door open as Ann went into the store. "Does Carlo have a favorite color?" she asked.

"When he steals my T-shirts, he seems to favor dark colors."

Ann chose a black T-shirt with white letters. Sean picked navy-blue with gray letters. She asked the clerk for a large.

"I'd go with extra large," Sean said. "Carlo is chubbier than he looks."

Ann stuck out her tongue. "Sean Miller, you are incorrigible."

"That's what everyone tells me, even my mother."

When they left the store, Sean said, "I know that you don't want company when you visit Carlo, but do you mind if I walk with you to the hospital? I'll spend a few minutes with Mr. Magnificent after you leave."

The request pleased her, although she wasn't sure why. She took a moment to form a reply that wouldn't communicate her feelings. "Actually, I'd appreciate your company, although you'll have to explain 'Mr. Magnificent' to me."

"That's what the production people at the Storm

Channel call Carlo when he can't hear them. On occasion, he behaves like he's the center of the universe."

"That doesn't surprise me. He is a rather special person," Ann said.

"True! Provided you define 'special' correctly." His expression became more mischievous. "I'll give you a tip for when you're chatting with Carlo. Whenever the conversation lags, begin to talk about him. It gets his attention every time."

Ann noticed that Sean's eyes seemed to gleam whenever he criticized Carlo, but so far he hadn't said anything that was genuinely mean-spirited. Sean's mild tirades seemed more begrudging than malicious. She reasoned that TV stars like Carlo were resented by their associates and subordinates. Carlo displayed the temperamental nature of a TV star, which meant that he was highly respected by the Storm Channel. Obviously, they put up with his foibles because he was good at what he did.

When they reached the hospital, Ann smiled at Sean. "Thanks for walking with me. I enjoyed your company." For a second, she thought she saw him blush, but he quickly said goodbye and headed off to the waiting room. She detoured to the gift shop and purchased the largest box of chocolate truffles they stocked. She tucked the Glory T-shirt beneath the chocolates in the bag, and took the elevator to the third floor.

Carlo was sitting up in bed watching TV when she entered his room. He looked even more handsome than when she'd first met him. The large white bandage had been replaced by a small black eye patch. It added an interesting hint of the exotic to his face, and he definitely resembled a heroic movie pirate.

"Huzzah!" he said, offering a slight bow. "Glory's dazzling church administrator has arrived, bearing gifts."

Ann couldn't help laughing at Carlo's corny compliment. He beamed at her, plainly pleased with her reaction to his greeting.

"How are you feeling?" she asked.

"Spectacular, now that you're here. You've brightened my whole day."

"What did the doctor say about your eye?" Ann asked, sitting in a chair positioned next to the bed.

"I've lost track of time. Today is Wednesday, right?"

"All day."

"The medics tell me that I've recovered sufficiently to leave the hospital this afternoon. I'll check in with my eye doctor again tomorrow. If I have his blessing, I'll fly back to New York City on Friday. That's where I live."

"Great! These will taste even better out of the hospital." She handed him the box of truffles.

He hefted the box. "Wow! You must have thought I'd be laid up for months."

"One can never possess too much chocolate."

"Remind me to propose to you one of these days! We think alike." He lifted the lid and chose a piece of candy. "I *love* dark chocolate."

Ann noted that he chewed the truffle with astonishing delicacy. Carlo was certainly one of the most graceful men she'd ever met. He maintained his elegance and dignity even in a hospital bed.

He went on, "I hope you realize that our makeup department won't be able to keep up with the zits these fat pills generate. If you see an ugly blotch on my face during a broadcast, know that you are personally responsible."

She shrugged theatrically. "I'll do my best to live with the guilt."

"Follow my approach. Never, ever pay attention to your

conscience. It can get in the way of your fun!" Carlo lifted the lid again and selected another truffle. "Fabulous! If I begin to display the symptoms of death by chocolate, please press the nurse-call button."

Ann gave the plastic bag a shake.

"Goodness!" Carlo said. "I hear something else. Don't tell me that you brought *two* presents."

"The truffles will soon be nothing but a fond memory." She unfolded the T-shirt and held it up. "But this is an enduring memento of Glory."

"I can't wait to wear it. Thank you, thank you, and thank you." Carlo used his remote control to switch off the TV. "I love the truffles and the shirt, Ann, but my fondest memories of Glory will always be of you."

Ann laughed, but warning bells rang in her head. Carlo's comment had been way over the top. He couldn't possibly expect her to take him seriously.

"Give the man with only one working eye a break," Carlo said. "You're sitting too far away from me. Come closer."

Ann pulled her chair closer to the side of Carlo's bed, then realized that she'd also moved out of her comfort zone.

Carlo patted the mattress. "Why don't you sit here with me?"

Ann swallowed a gasp of astonishment. She managed to say, "Thanks, but we'll both be more at ease if I stay in my own chair."

Carlo seemed unfazed by her refusal. "But if you don't sit down next to me, I won't be able to hold your hand."

Carlo leaned sideways faster than she could react and grasped her hand.

"You and I are soul mates. I knew that the first time I saw you."

She thought about pulling her hand loose, but she didn't want to insult or embarrass him.

"You strike me as a very caring person," he said. "You like to help people, don't you, Ann?"

The tone of his voice was making her feel awkward. Not knowing how else to answer his question, she nodded. "I try to help people whenever I can."

"We'll, you're in a position to help me and, in exchange, I can help you."

"How can I help you, Carlo?"

"I need a place to stay tonight and tomorrow night," he said, smiling his warmest smile.

"We have several charming B and B's in Glory," she said. "Sean is staying at the Scottish Captain. I'm sure they can accommodate you. They have delightful rooms, full of antique furniture."

"I was hoping for something more private."

"I'm not sure what you mean," Ann said, a feeling of dread creeping up her spine.

"What about your house, Ann? I saw a picture of it in Monday's newspaper. I'll bet you have a captivating guest room."

"Not really," she said, stunned at where Carlo was leading the discussion.

"What about a living room sofa? I'm not fussy about where I sleep. All that matters is that we're together tonight and tomorrow. We have so much to talk about—especially your television debut."

"My what?"

"I intend to put you on the Storm Channel and show you off to our millions of viewers. A lovely face like yours deserves to be on television!" He swept his free arm in a broad arc. "You'd make a dynamite weather girl." Carlo gazed at her with a startling intensity. "I find that the first step of working together effectively on the air is to become friends—intimate friends."

She felt her face begin to burn. Television debut? Intimate friends? *What does he think I am?*

"I couldn't possibly invite you into my home," she said. "That would be wholly inappropriate."

Carlo suddenly pulled Ann toward him.

Yikes! He's trying to kiss me!

The eruption of indignation that coursed through her body gave her the strength of ten. One quick yank broke Carlo's grip on her hand. For a delicious instant she thought about delivering a mighty slap to his cheek, but her good upbringing prevailed. How could she strike a man with a bandaged eye, lying in a hospital bed? Instead, she grabbed the box of truffles and the T-shirt, and fled toward the open door.

"Don't go!" Carlo shouted. He tried to stand up and his sheet slithered sideways, revealing a pair of knobby knees. She let herself laugh. The real Carlo Vaughn was less impressive than the TV personality—much less impressive.

Carlo fought with the sheet. "Give me another chance, Ann. You misunderstood me."

"*To the contrary,* Mr. Vaughn. I understand you perfectly. You're a class-A rat, a callous womanizer and an unmitigated lowlife. Be glad that I'm listening to my conscience right now. If I wasn't, I'd put your other eye out of commission."

Carlo's eyes lit up in anger. "Lighten up, lady. You lead a dull, hick-town life. I'm the most exciting thing that's happened to you in decades. You can't wait to tell your mind-numbing friends that Carlo Vaughn made a run at you. Of course, you'll leave out the crucial fact that I was half-blind at the time."

"You pompous, egotistical sleaze bucket!"

"Sticks and stones may break my bones, but leave the chocolate. I'm hungry."

She pushed the door closed before she could say something she'd regret, and made her way down the corridor to the visitor's lounge. True to his word, Sean was waiting inside.

"Why didn't you warn me about Carlo?"

"What happened?"

"What you knew would happen. I barely escaped his clutches!"

"Ah, well. Carlo can be relied upon to be Carlo," Sean said.

"You should've warned me what to expect."

"I told you he was a jerk."

"You didn't tell me he was a letch," Ann countered.

"First, I didn't think I had to. Carlo's reputation as a ladies' man is nationally known, well-deserved and reinforced by everything he says and does. Second, if I'd reported anything negative about Carlo, you wouldn't have listened to me."

"That's no excuse! You let me walk into his hospital room like a lamb to the slaughter," she said, turning and heading toward the stairway that led downstairs. She could hear Sean following her, and she was fairly certain that he was laughing.

Well, I deserved to be laughed at. I made a complete fool of myself.

But when she looked over her shoulder, she saw that he wasn't mocking her at all. If anything, his expression seemed gentle and tender.

Why is he looking at me that way?

"Don't be angry with me," Sean said. "I knew that you could take care of yourself. And you proved me right."

"That's only because my mother warned me years ago that a girl on her own can't trust a smooth-talking traveling man. Fortunately, I listened to her." She added, "I'll bet you and Carlo have women stashed in every town you broadcast from."

"Nah. Carlo's approach is so clumsy and obvious that intelligent females send him on his way, like you did. Me, on the other hand—I have dozens of lady friends from coast to coast."

Ann worried for an instant that it might be true. Sean's smile told her otherwise. "In your dreams!" she said.

Sean batted his eyelashes at her. "I'll have you know that women in every state are eager for my smooth-talking ways. But there just isn't enough of me to go around!"

"Shut up and eat a truffle," Ann said, trying not to smile. She thrust the box under his right arm. "I reclaimed them from Carlo. Along with the black T-shirt."

"That must have made him mad. He loves chocolate."

She nodded. "He was furious. Even his knobby knees were glowing red."

"You saw Carlo's knees?"

Ann began to laugh out loud and didn't catch her breath until they reached the hospital's lobby.

Bless you, Sean. I needed that.

One of the things that Sean liked best about Ann was that her face openly announced the way she felt. During the past several days, he'd seen her display a festival of emotions: fear, pleasure, worry, annoyance, delight, anger, amusement and now something else. It took him a moment to recognize that Ann, who had stopped laughing, had been thoroughly embarrassed by the wretched scene in Carlo's room.

Despite her shorter stride he had trouble keeping up

with her as she marched toward the Broad Street exit. She deftly sidestepped an elderly couple blocking her way, pushed through the revolving doors and disappeared from sight. He managed to catch up with her half a block away. He didn't need to see her face to know that she was chagrined and disappointed.

"Slow down, Ann." He moved alongside her and matched her pace. "Everyone has to learn the hard way about Carlo Vaughn. Don't blame yourself."

"Who else can I blame?" she said, still charging a step ahead of him along the sidewalk. "I feel like a cliché—a naive, small-town girl outwitted and outplayed by a handsome city slicker. I should have recognized from the get-go what Carlo was really after. He's a TV star and I'm a—"

"A marvelous woman who's much too charitable to recognize that Carlo is human pond scum. And a total pinhead, to boot," Sean said. Ann made a sound he couldn't decipher. "By the way," he continued, "nobody at the Storm Channel considers Carlo a TV star. To us, he's just a weather reporter." He took the box of chocolates from under his arm. "Would you like a truffle?"

"As a matter of fact, I would."

"Can we rest for a few seconds? I can't open the box while I'm speed walking."

She stopped and did a slow pirouette. Sean removed the lid and offered the box on his outstretched palm. She chose and devoured two dark-chocolate truffles.

"Yum."

"How about another?" he asked.

"Two of those delicious caffeine-filled puppies erased all memory of Carlo Vaughn. A third would merely keep me up all night."

"Good. I've had an idea."

"I'm not sure that I can handle any more male ideas this morning."

"Let's go see Rafe Neilson. We'll tell him my theory," Sean suggested.

"I've told you what will happen if you share your crazy ideas with Rafe."

"Actually, you didn't. You said that Rafe would ignore me. But I propose that we talk to him together."

"What difference will that make?"

"An enormous one, I predict. Together, we're two potential witnesses who have worthwhile insights about what actually happened to Richard Squires."

She shrugged. "I still think that Rafe will ignore us, but after my performance this morning, I probably owe you a favor. If you want me to tag along when you talk to Rafe, I will."

Sean and Ann spent most of their ten-minute stroll to police headquarters in silence. He enjoyed walking close to her and didn't want to risk ruining the moment. She remained equally quiet, lost in her own thoughts.

"What's your plan?" Ann finally said, as they turned right on Campbell Street. "Who does the talking?"

"Well, I suppose I should lay out my thinking. Then you can add your comments and observations."

"Fine. I'll try not to be my usual critical self."

Sean gave their names to the sergeant at the visitor's window who buzzed them through a door that led to the main bullpen. They found Rafe working at his desk. He seemed tired and wasn't wearing a complete uniform. Sean guessed that the deputy chief had been working flat out since Gilda passed overhead and hadn't had time to go home for a change of clothing. Rafe stood and welcomed them.

"I can give you five minutes, no longer. We're an officer short this morning." He gestured toward a pair of visitor's chairs near his desk. "Now, what have you two cooked up?"

Sean waited until Ann had slid into one of the chairs and then he took the other. But before he had a chance to speak, she started explaining.

"We came to see you, Rafe, because Sean has a theory about what happened to Richard Squires on Monday night. I urge you to listen to what Sean has to say, even though it may sound a bit weird."

Sean held his breath. *So much for our plan.*

But Rafe picked up a pen and slid a yellow notepad to his side of the desktop. "I'm all ears."

Sean relaxed and told Rafe about Richard's puzzling route through the parking lot, the unexpectedly neat position of his body under the rubble and the curious lack of damage to his face. "Taken together," he concluded, "these things suggest that Richard's death wasn't an accident and that someone killed him."

Rafe didn't interrupt him, nor did he say anything when Sean finished. Instead, he reached into a desk drawer and retrieved another yellow notepad, this one covered with writing.

"Here," he said. "Read my notes."

Sean read just a paragraph of scrawly handwriting. He pushed Rafe's notes toward Ann, stunned.

"Great minds think alike," Rafe said. "I identified the three suspicious facts you did, plus I came up with a fourth. I'd love to know what happened to Richard's hat that evening. Several people in the command center remember him wearing it that evening."

"Richard's hat!" Ann slapped her palm on the notepad.

"I'd forgotten about it. He *was* wearing a funny-looking baseball cap when he fixed the generator. It was bright red with a broad white brim that covered his face. I never saw the logo on the front, but I remember thinking that it was a crazy hat to wear during a hurricane because it didn't have a chin strap and the broad brim would catch the wind." She added, "Gilda probably blew Richard's hat halfway to Elizabeth City."

"What about my conclusions?" Sean lowered his voice. "Do you also think that Richard might have been murdered?"

"It's possible, though not probable," Rafe answered, softly. "I shouldn't tell you this, but the medical examiner's report is ambiguous. It doesn't say yes or no. All we really know for sure is that a blow to the back of the head killed Richard Squires. It's possible that the falling steeple hit Richard and created the bizarre circumstances you observed. Strange things happen during storms."

"Not *that* strange. It takes years of experience to become an expert on storm damage, but I've seen enough to recognize that someone gave Gilda the hurricane a helping hand, so to speak."

Rafe sighed. "Glory's leadership—our mayor, the chief of police and the director of emergency management—all accept that Richard Squires died in a freak accident. I'm not happy with that explanation—as we both know, too many of the details don't fit. And so, I've been dragging my feet, keeping the investigation open."

"Then you do agree with me," Sean said.

"Let's just say that the circumstantial evidence can be interpreted to suggest that Richard met with foul play." Rafe heaved another sigh. "But none of that makes any difference, because we don't have—"

"A motive," Ann interrupted. "There's no reason for anyone to kill Richard. I explained that to Sean, but he doesn't believe me."

Rafe leaned back in his chair. "Believe her, Sean. She's right. Without a good motive for murder I can't take the next step."

"What if I could find a legitimate motive?"

"You won't," Ann said. "Everyone loved Richard. He had no enemies."

"Yep," Sean said. "And the longer he's gone, the more popular he'll get."

Ann frowned. "That's a remarkably cynical attitude."

"I've never met Richard Squires," Sean said, "but I'm positive that he didn't die by accident. He may have been Glory's favorite son, but someone had a reason for wanting him dead."

Rafe leaned closer to Sean.

"I certainly can't encourage you to get involved," he said, his voice almost a whisper, "and I can't do anything to help you. But if you bring me even a puny motive suggesting why Richard might have been murdered, then I'll launch a full-scale investigation, no matter what the chief or anyone else in this town thinks."

Sean watched a look of astonishment spread across Ann's face. She was as surprised as he was that Rafe had given him a green light—of sorts.

"Please keep one caveat in mind," Rafe continued. "Dabbling with murder can be dangerous. If someone did kill Richard, that person won't have many qualms about killing you, should you become a perceived threat."

"Fortunately, he won't be working alone," Ann announced.

Sean immediately realized what Ann meant.

"No!" he said to her. "This is my project. I don't need any help."

Ann shook her head. "He doesn't know me very well," she said to Rafe.

"I guess not," Rafe replied with a laugh.

"Well, we'll let you get back to work." She held up the tactical police radio that dangled from the lanyard around her neck. "Do you want this back?"

"No. You'd better hang on to it. I'm always on the other end."

Sean asked himself how he'd lost control of the conversation. Actually, he'd never had it—Ann had taken charge and that was that. He rose without protest when she stood up, then followed her out of the bullpen. Sean looked back at Rafe, who shrugged and winked.

He wanted to talk with Ann about her intentions to work with him, but then he glanced at her face. The embarrassment he'd seen earlier was gone, leaving nothing but certitude and resolve.

That's a good thing, isn't it?

SEVEN

Ann left police headquarters startled at what she'd said and done. Why had she insisted on helping Sean? More to the point, when would she find the time to do it?

She'd made an open-ended commitment to work with Sean, but how much time did he intend to spend on his quest? He had nothing else to do for the next three days while waiting for his van to be repaired. But every minute she spent with him would take valuable time away from her responsibilities at Glory Community Church. How would she manage to search for Richard's killer and fight for her job at the same time? Had she taken on more than she should? Did she really have a choice?

Ann looked at her watch and groaned softly. She could almost feel all of Wednesday slipping away from her. It was a little past one o'clock. She'd planned to spend the afternoon at the church. Daniel hadn't ordered her back to work, but she knew that he needed her support. There were a thousand things that had to be done, from arranging for the plywood panels to be taken off the windows, to making sure the rehearsal room was ready for this evening's choir practice, to accommodating the dozens of organizations that routinely held meetings at the church, to organizing

Richard Squires's funeral, which was scheduled for Friday, to preparing a list of local folks who might need a helping hand with their recovery efforts…the list was endless.

I have problems, but so do hundreds of other people in Glory.

And then Ann remembered her mother. Her brother Alan planned to drive Mom back to Glory on Thursday. In other words, tomorrow! That created a new round of tasks for her. She'd need to put clean sheets on her mother's bed and the guest-room bed. And because they'd both be tired and hungry after the six-hour drive from Asheville, she'd have to find the time to get a hot supper ready for them. Before that, she'd need to restock the fridge, which she'd all but cleaned out in anticipation of Gilda causing a power outage.

Ann heard her stomach rumble.

"You sound as hungry as I feel," Sean said, his eyes bright with amusement.

"Sorry about that," she said. "I have noisy innards and I was thinking about food shopping."

"Why don't we stop for lunch before we go motive-hunting?"

"I really don't have the time for—" she began, but then her stomach rumbled again.

"You and your innards seem to have different opinions about your hunger."

"Trust me. I'll survive until dinner. I ate breakfast this morning, followed by two chocolate truffles."

"Even so, it won't take long to visit one of Glory's fast-food restaurants. Sharon, my nurse at the hospital, spoke glowingly about Snacks of Glory. She said that I had to try a SOGgy Burger before I left Glory."

Ann wanted to argue, but Sean's mention of a SOGgy

Burger sent another undeniable hunger pang through her midriff. In fact, her breakfast had been quick and meager—one small, frozen breakfast sandwich she'd nuked in her microwave.

"I'll be pleased to accompany you to Snacks of Glory," she said, "which is definitely one of Glory's special places. The SOGgy Burgers they serve are famous throughout the Carolinas. But let's not meander around town on foot. We'll hoof it to my house and pick up my car."

Ann led the way. They stopped at the intersection of Queen Street and Stuart Lane to allow a convoy of support trucks owned by the local cable TV company to pass. Ann considered the departing trucks one more sign of progress after the storm. The repair crews were leaving Glory, which meant that at least one downtown utility was back in service.

Ann chuckled to herself as she realized that Sean had taken on a similar mission of repair and recovery. There was only one way to get Phil Meade off her case. If Rafe could prove that Richard hadn't died accidentally, everything she had done—or not done—during that awful evening would become irrelevant. The first step on her road to redemption was to identify a potential motive for murder.

A new thought took over Ann's mind. Finding a motive was so important to her future that she didn't trust Sean to do it by himself. That's why she had insisted on coming along.

Here we are walking side by side like we're best buddies, but Sean doesn't know much about me, and I know even less about him. In fact, I haven't the vaguest idea why he's offered to help me. I mean, aside from the fact that he seems to like me. Not romantically, though. Or am I wrong about that? He's certainly been attentive.

When they reached Ann's house, Sean asked, "Wasn't your car inside your garage?"

"Yes, but the falling branch left my car unscathed— more's the pity." She laughed. "It's old, small and underpowered. I keep hoping for a reason to replace it, but it always starts and seems to run forever."

They climbed inside and she started the engine. "A quick lunch and then we hunt for a motive."

"Sounds like a strategy," Sean said.

"You haven't explained what you intend to do this afternoon. How does one look for a reason to kill another person? I have no idea." She slipped the car in gear. "Did that textbook you browsed through provide any guidance?"

"As a matter of fact, it did. There are four leading motives for murder. Greed—murder prompted by love of money or a related form of covetousness; jealousy— murder driven by possessiveness; revenge—murder to get even; and self-protection—murder to prevent the revelation of past acts or deeds."

"That's a nasty list," Ann said, "but none of those items fit the Richard Squires I knew."

"You're focused on the wrong thing, Ann. Even though Richard was an all-around nice guy, someone else in Glory may have been jealous of him, fearful of him, committed to getting even with him or determined to separate him from his money. To figure out why Richard was murdered, we need to understand his life, his relationships, and his business dealings."

Ann had to admit that his reasoning rang true. "So where do we begin?"

"If I say 'Richard Squires,' what leaps into your mind?"

"Squires' Place, of course," Ann answered.

"So let's start there. Then we tug on any threads that might lead to more useful information."

"That seems easier in theory than practice," she said. "I wish we knew more about detecting than what you've read in a textbook."

"We'll learn as we go."

"If you say so, Sherlock."

"I do, Watson. Trust me."

Less than five minutes later, Ann parked her venerable compact sedan on Oliver Street, next to Snacks of Glory.

"Remind me to take a picture of that neon sign." Sean pointed at the glowing hamburger—mostly red and yellow—hanging in the front window. "It's so delightfully tasteless."

"Do you enjoy being a snob?" Ann asked, smiling.

"You're the one who was impressed by Carlo Vaughn!"

"Okay." Ann laughed. "We're both snobs. Please don't mention him again."

Ann guided Sean inside. More than half of the dozen or so tables were occupied, but Ann's favorite table—a round two-seater tucked into the back corner—was vacant.

"Hi, Ann," a waitress called from the middle of the dining area. "Do you need a menu today?"

"Not today, not ever. We'll each have a Deluxe SOGgy Burger and a sweet tea."

The waitress gave a mock salute. "On the way!"

"Hmm. You're sure about that iced tea thing?" Sean said. "Up north, we usually drink soda with our burgers."

"Unthinkable! You're in North Carolina now. A SOGgy Burger without sweet tea is like a day without sunshine."

A grin crossed his face. "In that case, thank you for preventing a gullible Yankee from committing a cultural crime. Speaking of crime," he said, "tell me about Rafe Neilson. He seems more...uh, sophisticated than other small-town cops I've met."

"Rafe is as sharp as they come. He used to be a special investigator with the New York State Police. Daniel says that Glory is lucky to have him."

His smile became thoughtful. "Yeah, but is he protective of the locals? Is he likely to shy away from conducting an investigation that might implicate a leading Glory resident?"

"I trust Rafe. If he says he'll do something, he'll do it, even if it means rocking Glory's boat."

Ann moved her silverware to one side as the waitress arrived with two overflowing plates and two vast glasses of sweet tea.

"That's got to be the biggest burger in all Creation," Sean said.

"Not even close." The waitress scooped up a few fries that had slipped off the plates. "Our Humongous SOGgy Burger is twice as large."

"Thanks for the warning." He waited until the waitress left and then asked Ann, "Shall I give the blessing?"

"Uh...great!" Ann said, startled by the question.

Sean took her hand. "Heavenly Father, we thank You for the fellowship around this table and Your provision of these delicious SOGgy Burgers. Please bless them to our use and us to Your service. And help us both make wise choices in the days ahead. In Jesus' name we pray. Amen."

"Amen," Ann repeated, trying to keep the astonishment she felt out of her voice. She hadn't expected Sean to be openly Christian—or be able to pray so confidently.

Her own Christian walk had developed a pothole or two in recent years. God had allowed things to happen that bewildered her. She could still talk a good game about her faith, but her doubts had increased, although she'd never admit that to anyone. A big reason for taking her job at Glory Community Church had been to reconnect with God.

I know You're out there, but something is wrong with our relationship.

"Pardon me!" Sean said, hastily releasing her hand and lunging for the ketchup. Only then did she become aware that he had continued to hold her hand for several seconds after finishing the blessing. Even more surprising, she'd enjoyed the touch of his fingers on hers.

She saw a blush travel up Sean's cheeks. Moreover, his flurry of activity with his SOGgy Burger seemed more designed to hide his embarrassment than to eat lunch.

Ann swallowed a laugh. Something was going on here, but neither of them was saying anything. They both had lots to learn about candor.

Maybe we both need to speak our minds.

A sermon Daniel had recently preached sprung to mind. "God knows your hearts," Daniel had said. "And he knows what you're thinking." Ann dug her cell phone out of her purse.

"I hate people who make calls in a restaurant," she said to Sean, "but since we have our own quiet corner, I want to call Daniel and tell him what I'm doing."

"Don't worry about me—I'm busy," he said, after he polished off a big bite of his burger.

She pressed the D-for-Daniel speed-dial key. "Daniel. It's Ann."

"Are you feeling better?"

"Much, but I won't be back at church until three o'clock. I'm sorry, but—"

"No need to explain. I had lunch with Rafe. I approve of what you and Sean are doing. Rafe's impressed with him, says that he's a good man to have on your side."

"I'm beginning to think so, too," Ann said, sneaking a peek at Sean as he ate.

"Take as much time as you need. I'll put out a call for volunteers to help with the routine administrative details."

She thanked him and ended the call.

"You have a strangely faraway smile on your face," Sean said.

"Daniel Hartman is an awe-inspiring person. And the best, most understanding boss I've ever had. You'll have to meet him sometime, Sean."

She ate as much of her SOGgy Burger as she could manage. When they'd both finished, she said, "Sean, can I ask you a question?"

"Uh, sure." He nodded stiffly, amplifying the deer-in-the-headlights gaze that delivered a contrary answer.

Ann decided to press on. "I've been pondering—why are you so keen to help me?" Without thinking it through, she added, "What's in it for you?"

Sean's clear brown eyes seemed to double in size. "Wow! You called me cynical today, but you're the East Coast distributor of cynicism." His face filled with disappointment. "How can you ask me that?"

Ann squirmed at her own tactlessness. "That came out wrong. I didn't mean to insult you or question your sincerity. I'm grateful for your help, but I don't understand why you put yourself on my team. Why take a risk—and maybe endanger your life—for someone you met two days ago, especially when you plan to leave in two more days?" She leaned forward and touched his hand. "I'm confident that you don't have the same short-term game plan as Carlo Vaughn."

She'd hoped that her combined apology and clarification would calm his obvious annoyance, but all it accomplished was to magnify the miffed scowl that dominated his expression.

He paused several seconds to frame his reply. "I admire you and I dislike Phil Meade. Let's leave it at that."

Ann struggled to find a graceful way out of the awkward situation she'd created, but in the end she settled on saying nothing more. Once again, she'd spoken words to Sean that she wished she could withdraw. What could explain this? Certainly not her anxiety about Phil Meade. If that were the root cause, she'd have this issue with everyone, but the problem seemed limited to Sean. Why would that be?

No doubt about it—I need to do some heavy-duty thinking about my feelings for Sean Miller.

Sean stared through the windshield, knowing that if he looked at Ann he might yell at her. True, she'd apologized for her hurtful question. But he needed more time to cool down—and fully forgiving her thoughtless words would take even more time.

"Where are we?" he asked.

"Approaching Albemarle Sound, about to turn south on Front Street." She sniffed the air. "What's that rank smell?"

"The unmistakable odor of flooded house," he replied. "The owners have begun to clear away water-damaged furnishings."

"You're right. Look!"

Sean saw piles of waterlogged carpet and water-soaked furniture stacked at the ends of driveways. The windows of the affected houses were wide open and, at several, engine-powered blowers were chugging away, ventilating crawl spaces.

"Oh, my goodness!" Ann stopped unexpectedly in front of a blue clapboard Victorian bungalow. "This is where Rafe and Emma live. It used to be the prettiest house in Glory."

"It will be again once the gingerbread trim is replaced. That kind of wind damage is easy to fix. The most serious harm was caused by the storm surge. I'm guessing a mini-tsunami rolled up the embankment, punched through the front door and windows, and probably took out most of the first floor."

"Poor Rafe. We bent his ear about my troubles when he has all of this on his mind. Now I feel like a jerk," Ann said.

"Would you like a second opinion about that?"

She laughed. "Are you still mad at me?"

"Not as much as I was a minute ago. It's hard to stay angry about a few ill-chosen words when Rafe manages to be gracious to the likes of us while dealing with this mess."

She accelerated away from the curb. "Squires' Place is on Main Street, next to the Bank of Glory."

"That's near the heart of downtown Glory?"

"Yup. It's been there for more than forty years."

"There it is," Sean said, as soon as Ann turned west on Main Street. "There's even a parking spot out front."

"There's also a Closed sign hanging in the front door. We've met our first detecting challenge."

"Let's see what's going on. One of us should read all the writing on the sign."

"That would be you," she said. "I'll keep the engine running."

The two structures on the block—the Bank of Glory and Squires' Place—were both substantial stone-faced buildings that must have been built at the same time. Sean walked quickly to Squires' Place as if hurrying would make the restaurant less closed.

He read the small print on the sign: "Squires' Place will remain closed out of respect for Richard Squires until after his funeral on Friday. We will reopen on Saturday at 5:00 p.m. for dinner."

He looked around. Perhaps someone had posted an In an emergency, call… notice. No joy. He cupped his hands around his face and peered through the front window.

He jogged back to Ann's car. "We may not have to rethink our strategy," he said. "I saw a light in back and shadows moving. There's someone in the restaurant after all."

"Is there a rear entrance?"

"I think so. Trucks probably don't deliver to the front door."

"How do we find it?"

"Start driving around the block."

The only alley on Front Street served the Bank of Glory, but one of the two alleys on Campbell Street led to the rear of Squires' Place, and a stoutly made steel door.

Sean rang the doorbell. He heard footsteps approaching and stepped back in anticipation. The door swung open, revealing a slender, tall and attractive woman he guessed to be in her late forties. She had reddish-blond hair piled high on her head and big brown eyes accented by heavy eye makeup.

"Oh," Ann said, behind him. "Sheila…" Ann hesitated. "I'm sorry, but I've forgotten your last name."

"Sheila Parker," the woman replied. "I have a terrible memory for names, too. You're Ann *somebody* from the church."

"Ann Trask." She moved in front of Sean and extended her hand.

"It's all coming back," Sheila said. "The last time we

worshipped at Glory Community, Richard mentioned that
you were the new church administrator."

"And I remember you," Ann said. "You accompanied
Richard on several Sundays as a visitor."

"I loved to hear Richard sing. He had a beautiful voice.
I could pick him out from the rest of the choir."

"Can we talk to you about Richard?"

"Absolutely! I prayed that someone from the church
would finally contact me, and here you are." She stepped
back from the door and moved into a corridor that, Sean
presumed, led deeper into the restaurant. "Please, come
inside. We'll be more comfortable in Richard's office."

"Uh…thank you," Ann said with a hesitant stammer.
Sean guessed that Ann didn't know what Sheila wished to
talk about or why she might want someone from Glory
Community to contact her.

Ann stopped short, causing Sean to bump into her.
"Forgive my manners," she said to Sheila. "Let me introduce Sean Miller. Sean is visiting Glory this week and has
offered to help me resolve a few problems. Do you mind
if he listens while we chat?"

The woman broke into a pained grimace that Sean
found disconcerting. "Certainly not, dear. Now that
Richard is dead, I have no secrets anymore. It's high time
that everyone in Glory knew the truth about our relationship."

Ann glanced at him over her shoulder. The puzzled
look on her face spoke volumes.

They followed Sheila into the restaurant's spacious
interior. The walls were paneled with wood planking alternately painted bright white and dazzling red. Sean es-
timated the main dining room could seat 150 people—in
four- and six-person booths that lined the walls and at

several dozen square wooden tables, also painted white and trimmed with red. The chairs and the booth benches were upholstered in shiny red vinyl that echoed the trim color. "This is what it would feel like," Sean muttered, "to live inside a candy cane."

Several framed posters on the wall reiterated the red-and-white theme. Bright red crockery sitting on stark white counters displayed Squires' Place's colorful dishes. Signs on the wall above the counters served as menus.

Red-Bowl Cheesy Shrimp and Grits—the Dish that Made Squires' Place Famous

Red-Bowl Grits and Red-Eye Gravy—Better than Your Momma Served You

Red-Bowl Grits—No One on Earth Serves Better Grits (We're Sure We Have the Angels Beat, Too)

Red-Bowl Sausage Grits—Yummy in the Tummy! Accept no Substitutes!

A large sign above the swinging door to the kitchen proclaimed, Grits and Glory: Made for Each Other.

Sheila led them down a corridor, past the Gritty Guy's Room, to a door marked Private.

"This is Richard's office," she said. "Don't mind the mess. Untidiness was his only failing, but he managed to find anything he needed."

She opened the door and flipped a light switch, revealing a good-size office furnished with a large wooden desk, a credenza, several bookcases, an overstuffed sofa and three ancient-looking recliners.

Sean studied the large watercolor on the wall behind the sofa. A rather amateurish artist had painted a curiously distorted view of the interior of Squires' Place.

"Ah. You've noticed the painting," Sheila said. "Richard loved it. His daughter Erin painted it fifteen years ago."

"Charming," Sean said.

The "mess" that Sheila had warned them about was a vast pile of paper on Richard's desk. There must have been hundreds of file folders, paper documents and brochures in ten different stacks. Sean grinned at the muddle; his desk was often just as cluttered.

Sheila pointed toward a corner. "That door leads to a file room, but Richard rarely took the time to file anything. Most of his filing cabinets are half-full. Sit anywhere you like," Sheila said. She sat in one of the visitor's chairs placed next to Richard's desk. Ann made for the plush sofa and Sean sat next to her.

"What a lovely photo," Ann said, picking up a shiny silver frame that perched on the end table next to the sofa.

"Isn't it," Sheila agreed. "Richard and I went on Glory Community's trip to the Outer Banks in July."

"And such a beautiful frame." She handed it to Sean.

Sean studied the photo. The well-composed eight-by-ten showed Richard and Sheila happily holding hands, standing in front of a sand dune, a lighthouse in the distance. Sean realized that this was the first good picture of Richard he'd seen. The anonymous photographer had captured the enthusiasm that Sean kept hearing about, and the love of life. Conversely, the grainy image that the *Glory Gazette* had published made Richard look old and tired—a man bored with the world.

"I didn't know that you were *more* than close friends," Ann said.

"It shows in that photo, doesn't it?" She pulled a handkerchief from her sleeve and dabbed an eye.

Ann nodded; Sheila continued. "Richard wanted to

marry me, but we never told anyone about our relationship."

"You were engaged?" Ann said.

"Not quite. He'd asked, but I hadn't accepted. I insisted that we be sensible."

"I'm not sure I understand," Ann said.

"Richard was twenty years older than me. He was a successful businessman, I was one of his employees, the hostess in his restaurant. I feared what would happen if we announced our engagement too quickly. I knew that some might see me as a gold digger."

Sean wasn't surprised by her concerns. A town the size of Glory would have its share of gossips willing to believe that a good-looking hostess had led Richard down the garden path.

Sheila continued, "I insisted that we move slowly, let people see us together, give them a chance to know me and to discover how much we loved each other." She dried her eyes again. "I was also concerned about how his grown children would feel, having a stepmother so much younger than their father. We planned to travel to Texas early in the new year and tell them in person."

Ann jumped in. "I know that Pastor Hartman has spoken with Richard's children. They've arranged the details of the funeral."

"I don't want to be pushy," Sheila said, "but I have information to contribute. Richard talked about his wishes with me." She waved her hands, as if to erase what she'd just said. "We didn't talk about the kind of funeral he wanted, but about the hymns he wanted sung. He joked about it. He said that without him singing, there were only three hymns the choir could perform well."

"That's an easy issue to resolve," Ann said. "I'll ask

Nina McEwen, our choral director, to call you. You and she can work out which hymns the choir will sing on Friday."

"That would be wonderful, dear." Sheila started to smile but then began to weep. "Oh, how I wish we'd been less sensible," she said between sobs. "If we'd married like he wanted to, Richard might have gone to Rocky Mount with me on the night he…" Sheila couldn't continue for a moment.

Ann waited for her to regain herself and then asked, "When did you meet Richard?"

"Shortly after I moved to Glory," Sheila said. "That would be about six months ago. Richard needed a hostess, I needed a job. He often said the timing was providential—clearly God driven."

Sean was about to ask where she'd moved from, but Sheila told the story without further prompting.

"I used to live in York, Pennsylvania. Last winter was a particularly snowy one, and I was becoming tired of the cold. I read about Glory in my dentist's waiting room. *Southern Living Magazine* had a lovely article about the town. The pictures I saw of Glory intrigued me and my first visit sold me on the town. It's pretty, charming and delightfully Southern, but in a way that doesn't overwhelm a Northerner like me. I knew that Glory would be a great place to live within minutes of driving past the welcome sign."

"How brave," Ann said. "I'm not sure I'd have the courage to make a decision like that."

Sheila beamed, thrilled by Ann's compliment. "My husband died five years ago. It took me all that time to find the guts to leave York. After all, my friends were there, I had a good job and I felt secure." She smiled again. "But I truly believe, as did Richard, that God wanted me in North Carolina. So here I am."

"What will you do now, Sheila?" Sean asked. "Will you stay in Glory?"

Sheila shrugged. "I don't know, but it's the question I ask every time I pray. Richard wasn't sure whether he would continue to live in Glory, actually. We talked about moving closer to the ocean, possibly to Manteo or Beaufort."

"Richard thought about leaving Glory?" Ann's voice proclaimed her surprise.

"It wasn't definite," Sheila said. "He liked to daydream about the different things he could do after he sold Squires' Place."

"That's something else I hadn't heard," Ann said, glancing at Sean.

"Of course you didn't. Mr. Hayden swore Richard to secrecy for business reasons. He would be furious if he knew that Richard had told me the little he did. But now, it doesn't matter. The deal is off because Richard's dead."

"Who is Mr. Hayden?" Ann asked.

"An urban developer. Didn't I say?" Sheila answered.

"Did he intend to buy Squires' Place?" Sean asked.

"Yes, but not to run as a restaurant. Mr. Hayden is some sort of urban developer. As near as I could understand, he planned to tear down this building and build a new office complex. But I don't know any of the details."

"Is Mr. Hayden based in Glory?"

"No. He's from Norfolk, Virginia, as I recall." Sheila dabbed at her eyes again.

"Thank you for talking to us, Sheila," Ann said. "We've taken up enough of your time. And if I don't get back to the church in five minutes, Pastor Hartman will turn me into a pumpkin."

Sean pushed himself out of the sofa's deep cushions and helped to pull Ann free.

"I'll make sure that Nina McEwen calls you," she said. They said their goodbyes to Sheila, and Sean followed Ann to her car.

"We're making progress," he said, "I smell a possible motive. Look around—Squires' Place is sitting on prime Glory real estate. The land Richard owned is too valuable to use as the site of a restaurant. Had the deal gone through, Richard would suddenly have been a wealthy man. Money can generate a gazillion reasons to kill someone."

"I agree, but the deal hadn't gone through. Now his kids will inherit the property. Why kill Richard *before* he becomes rich?"

"First things first—we need to talk to this Hayden guy as soon as we can." He clicked his seat belt and Ann started the engine. "By the way, what did you think of Sheila Parker?"

"I get suspicious of anyone who calls me 'dear.'"

"I'll take that under advisement," Sean said.

Ann laughed. He felt his face getting red and hoped that she wouldn't notice.

EIGHT

The streetlamps on Broad Street flickered off as Ann stood on the sidewalk outside the Scottish Captain, waiting for Sean to emerge. She felt a fresh stab of guilt at the thought that Sean was about to make yet another sacrifice for her.

Somewhere deep inside the B and B, Emma Neilson and her breakfast chef were hard at work preparing one of the finest breakfasts in the Carolinas. Alas, Sean would miss breakfast so that he could accompany her on a visit to Mr. Hayden.

After they'd left Squires' Place the previous afternoon, Sean had gone online to locate the Hayden Development Corporation in Norfolk. Miles Hayden, its president, agreed to meet with Sean and Ann at 8:45 a.m. the next morning. "Any later is impossible," Hayden had said, "because of my pressing schedule." They would need to be on the road by 6:45 a.m.—long before the Scottish Captain began serving breakfast.

It had rained during the night, leaving small puddles in the sidewalk's uneven surface. Now that the sun was up, Ann could see a distorted reflection of herself in the nearest puddle—and various bits of tiny flotsam like a flotilla of

tiny boats. She kicked at the puddle with her shoe and—
for the umpteenth time that morning—tried to sort out her
feelings for Sean.

He'd made every effort to be kind, generous and caring.
He'd also offered considerable evidence that he liked and
admired her. And maybe—just maybe—she was beginning
to feel the same way about him. But today was Thursday
and Sean planned to leave Glory on Saturday—an insur-
mountable stumbling block to building an ongoing relationship.

*Why warm to a man who would soon evaporate with-
out a trace?*

She looked up when she heard a door shut. Sean was
walking toward her cradling a white paper bag in his arms.
"A gift from Emma," he said. "Hot coffee and warm sweet
rolls. We won't go hungry during our journey to Norfolk."

She started her car; he climbed in beside her. "It should
be a pleasant drive this morning," she said.

"Then what say we open the sunroof?" Sean suggested.
"We'll enjoy an alfresco breakfast while we drive north."

She watched Sean stretch his legs as far as the sedan's
compact interior would allow. She envied him—he seemed
relaxed, confident. She, though, felt glum and on edge,
almost certain that their visit to Miles Hayden would yield
nothing of value. If Richard Squires had no obvious
enemies in Glory, why should he make one seventy miles
away in Norfolk?

Ann thought about ending the futile trip before it began
and sending Sean back to his breakfast, but she knew that
he would refuse. He seemed convinced that they were onto
something.

When they were clear of Glory, she pulled to the
shoulder for a few moments so that they could enjoy the

coffee and sweet rolls. Both were delicious. Sean seemed pleased that she enjoyed them.

"I bring interesting news along with the grub," he said. "Carlo Vaughn leaves Glory forever this morning. He spent last night at the Glory House on King Street. The Storm Channel rustled up a limousine to drive him to the Norfolk airport."

"We could have taken him with us."

"That didn't strike me as a great idea, although the conversation would have been fascinating and poor Carlo would have needed additional medical care," Sean teased.

"Poor Carlo, my foot! It's a pity that I didn't get a chance to say a proper goodbye."

"Oh, but he thinks you did. He told me what you said to him at the hospital. Word for word. Did you really call him an 'unmitigated lowlife'?"

"I believe I did. But my favorite part of the tirade was 'pompous, egotistical sleaze bucket.'" Ann cringed when she recalled her out-of-whack first impression of Carlo Vaughn. Why, she asked herself, had she thought Carlo so much more handsome than Sean? He may have been more photogenic, but his perfect features were an empty facade for his pinhead intellect and would soon grow boring. By contrast, Sean's rugged asymmetrical face mirrored his considerable intelligence, and became more interesting each time she looked at him.

Sean patted his shirt pocket. "I have detailed directions to Hayden's office, in case you need them."

"Thanks, but I know how to get to Bank Street. I frequently shop in Norfolk." She didn't say that she'd made the trip so often that she knew the way by heart. "Miles Hayden's office is less than a mile from Nauticus."

"What's Nauticus?"

"A nifty maritime-themed science museum. My guess is you'd love it. I went along with a group of church members last year. We saw a great exhibition on navigation. Afterward we took a boat ride around the harbor. Norfolk Naval Station is the largest navy base in the world. The U.S. Navy has seventy-five ships based there."

"My job took me to Norfolk last year. All I saw was Town Point Park and a small patch of the James River. Sounds like I missed a lot."

"Um, since you brought it up, can I ask a question about your job?"

"Sheesh! Not another personal question."

"I'll try not to insult you again, but to prepare for every eventuality, I'll apologize in advance."

"I accept your apology in advance. Ask away."

"I know that you work for the Storm Channel, but I don't know what you do other than drive a big van. I assume that you have a few other, more challenging responsibilities."

Sean laughed. "I'm what the Storm Channel calls a field producer. I do everything from overseeing remote broadcasts and handling all the logistics to taking care of travel arrangements, setting up the equipment, driving the van and, when necessary, serving as Carlo Vaughn's valet."

"How long have you been a field producer?"

"Four long, dull years. Two of them Carlo-drenched."

"Yikes. They must pay you vast sums of money," Ann said.

"Vast enough to make a dent in my student loans. I owed a ton of cash when I finished my meteorology degree at the University of Miami." He toasted her with his coffee cup. "What about you? Where did you go to school? Is there a college that specializes in church administrating?"

"I attended East Carolina University in Greenville. My degree is in business administration. I earn a modest sum, but I'm happy working at Glory Community Church."

Happier than I've been in a long, long time.

"Hmm. You don't look like a B-school type to me. You're much too nice to be a hardheaded manager."

She knew that Sean meant to flatter her, but with his compliment had surfaced an unhappy memory she'd rather have left buried. She decided not to explain that business had been her second choice, that she'd actually started college as an education major, on her way to being a grade-school teacher.

"I'm tougher than I look," she replied, "and nasty to the core."

"Not!" Sean said.

She laughed. "Don't say I didn't warn you."

At eight o'clock they crossed the Berkeley Bridge and arrived in downtown Norfolk. Five minutes later, Ann located a parking space close to the Chesapeake Commercial Center, a fifteen-story glass and steel office building. The directory in the marble-floored lobby announced that the Hayden Development Corporation was on the seventh floor, in suite 703.

"I'm beginning to recognize the different expressions on your face," Sean said as they boarded the elevator. "I currently see skepticism. Please explain."

Ann pushed seven and the doors slid shut. "Senior executives usually have full calendars. I'm astonished that Miles Hayden agreed to see us on such short notice."

"Undoubtedly because I'm remarkably persuasive on the telephone."

"That must be it."

"Oh, ye of little faith," Sean countered.

The elevator doors whooshed open. "Lead on," Ann said.

Suite 703 was at the end of a long corridor. Sean turned a bronze doorknob and pushed open the door.

Ann walked in and saw a stocky man standing next to a receptionist's workstation. He was of medium height, in his early fifties and wore a fairly obvious toupee.

"You must be Ann Trask," he said. "I'm Miles Hayden. My secretary is ill today, so I'm the only one on duty this morning." He extended his hand.

"I'm pleased to meet you, Mr. Hayden," she said.

"I presume you're Sean Miller."

"Yes, indeed." Sean shook Hayden's hand after Ann released it.

"I can't offer you coffee," Hayden said. "Unfortunately, only my secretary knows how to do that. That being so, let's get down to business." He sat on a small sofa at the front of the reception area and waved at two facing steel-and-leather chairs. "Make yourselves comfortable."

When Ann and Sean were seated, Hayden said, "When you called yesterday, you said you wanted to talk about Richard Squires. But you also said that neither you nor Ann is next of kin."

"Correct," Ann said. "I'm Administrator at Glory Community Church and Sean is—"

"No need to explain yourselves," he interrupted. "I have several friends in Glory and I checked you out." He smiled. "Let's save time and cut right to the chase. Only one person in Glory could have told you about me—Sheila Parker. A not-so-bright lady with big hair and an even bigger mouth. Richard deserved better, but that's all water under the bridge." He continued. "You obviously want to know what kind of business arrangement I had going with Richard, am I right?"

Ann nodded. "You're right."

"Well, I have a proposition. I need a favor—a small one, but important nonetheless. You help me and I'll help you. I don't have to tell you that that's the way things get done in the world of business."

"What kind of favor?" Ann asked.

"Richard Squires's children will attend his funeral tomorrow."

"Jordan and Erin?" she said.

"Mr. Jordan Squires and Mrs. Erin Squires Bradshaw," Hayden laughed. "Checking me out? Huh? Did I pass your test?"

"With an A-plus."

"I've arranged to meet with them before the ceremony begins. We need a room at the church. Someplace quiet and private, where we won't be disturbed." He smiled at Ann. "Do you have an office?"

Ann's fists clenched involuntarily. She relaxed them and hoped that Hayden hadn't noticed. It took every ounce of her self-control to avoid telling him what she thought of someone who wanted to talk business at a funeral.

"Have Jordan and Erin agreed to this meeting?" she asked.

"Absolutely. Call them if you don't believe me."

"Then I have no objection to *them* using my office."

"And I have no objection to telling you what I cooked up with Richard Squires." He chuckled. "Cooked up—get it?"

Ann gritted her teeth. "I get it."

"Well, our plan was to rip down Squires' Place, clear the whole half block next to the Bank of Glory, and erect a ten-story office building. The Hayden Professional Center will attract high-value service businesses to Glory—law firms, financial planners, accounting firms, advertising agencies—the kind of companies that will provide the growth that Glory needs. My plan calls for specialty shops on the first floor, and a rooftop restaurant that offers a spectacular view of Albemarle Sound."

"I see. You intend to move Squires' Place to the roof."

"No, no, no. The Hayden Professional Center will have a world-class eatery on top, not a hayseed grits joint with cockamamie red-and-white walls. I promised Richard we'd find another location in downtown Glory for a new and improved Squires' Place."

"So Richard didn't intend to leave Glory…gritless?" Sean inquired.

"Are you kidding? That restaurant was his baby. Richard really thought that he served the best grits in the South—as if such a ludicrous thing as 'best grits' were possible." He frowned. "What are grits, anyway?"

"Stone-ground corn," Ann answered. "The finer part is called corn meal, the coarser part is called grits. The simplest recipe is to pour the grits into boiling water and then simmer, stirring occasionally, until the grits absorb the water. That's the kind of grits you get for breakfast in the Grits Belt."

"The what?" Sean asked.

"Louisiana to North Carolina."

"You learn something exciting every day," Hayden said dryly.

"Do you know that grits is the official prepared food of Georgia?" Ann asked.

Hayden shrugged. "And tell me why I should care?"

"Moving right along," Sean said, sensing Ann's anger. "Do Jordan and Erin know about your development scheme?"

"That's why we're meeting tomorrow. They're Richard's

heirs. Once they give me the okay, I'll move ahead with the planning phase."

"Do they intend to rebuild Squires' Place after you demolish the building?"

"Beats me, but if they do, they're on their own. Frankly, I'm way too busy to worry about a small-town restaurant." Ann noticed that Hayden made a point of looking at his watch. "I have to get back to work. I want to be ready to go the instant the court probates Richard's will."

"Thank you for your time," Sean said. "I'm really excited by your plans for little Glory."

"And so you should be. My new building will kick-start Glory's lagging economy. Tourist trade is okay, but nothing brings in money like a revitalized downtown."

Ann and Sean rose from their seats and said their goodbyes. They walked side-by-side along the corridor, not saying anything until the elevator was on its way down.

"Were you impressed by Hayden?" she asked.

"Not especially. I don't buy his my-secretary-is-sick-today story. His office looked sparse. If he's a real-estate developer, he's not a very successful one."

"You can't judge that kind of book by its cover, though. Hayden may be having short-term cash-flow problems, but if he has the right contacts, he can still marshal enough resources to put together a major business deal in Glory."

"Assuming that he told us the truth."

"Well, what do you think?" she said. "Did you believe Hayden?"

"Here and there, but not everywhere. I've organized so many interviews with devious local politicians that I've learned how to read body language. Some of what he said is truthful—he needs your office to meet with Richard's children, for example. But Miles Hayden has his own agenda and he didn't tell us the whole truth."

"Great. We're still at square one," she said.

She looked away from Sean and willed herself to stay calm. *Sean is trying to help me. It's not his fault that we're not making any progress.*

Ann seemed completely lost in thought when they reached her sedan. Without any warning, she lobbed the car keys at him. "You drive!" she ordered.

"Yes, your highness." He punctuated his reply with a curtsy, but she ignored his feeble attempt at humor. He could feel the frustration coming off her in waves.

He unlocked the car. She sprang into the passenger's seat then yanked the door shut with enough force to rock the compact sedan on its springs.

Sean climbed into the driver's seat, started the engine and aimed the rearview mirror so he could see her face. She'd pressed her head against the headrest, her eyes shut, her expression bleak. But despite her grim visage, there was color in her cheeks, and she looked remarkably pretty.

"You are a strange lady, Ann Trask," he murmured, as he readjusted his mirror and pulled into traffic.

"Did you say something?" she asked.

"I said 'You are a strange lady, Ann Trask.'"

"What are you talking about?"

"You…and me," he said.

"Sean, you're babbling."

"You seem angry, Ann. Was it something I did?"

"I'm not mad at you. I'm mad at me—and at the situation."

"What situation, Ann?"

"What situation?"

"Just call me Blockhead Miller," he said.

Ann began to smile. "I'm sorry, Sean, but I'm wound tighter than a broken alarm clock."

"I'd never have noticed," he said. "Are you going to tell me why?"

She sighed. "Look. We drove all the way from Glory to Norfolk to find a reason why someone might want to kill Richard Squires, but we still don't have a motive." She sighed again. "When I think of all the work waiting for me back at the church, well, I feel stupid for wasting an entire morning on a meeting with a man we both agree was less than truthful with us."

"Look at the bright side. We've learned many new facts about Richard Squires during the past twenty-four hours."

"But not the most important fact."

"Well, you know what they say about detecting."

"As a matter of fact, I have no idea." Ann laughed.

"Eighty percent of the work done during an investigation doesn't pay off. The trouble is, no one knows in advance which eighty percent not to do. In other words, we may have made a vital discovery, but we just don't realize it yet."

"A lot of good that's going to do me. I'm running out of time, Sean."

The intensity of Ann's voice—the anxiety her tone conveyed—stunned Sean. Several seconds passed before he realized what she'd actually said.

"Running out of time?" he asked "In what way? Rafe didn't give us a specific deadline to meet."

"Forget it. Now I'm babbling."

"I don't want to forget it. You're concerned about time and I want to know why," he said gently.

She hesitated before she replied. "Well, you're going to

leave Glory soon, and then I'll be investigating on my own."

Sean glanced at her and realized instantly that Hayden wasn't the only one being less than truthful.

She's lying to me. Why?

Sean gripped the steering wheel tightly and wondered what to do next.

He tried to recall their conversation after they'd left Miles Hayden. At first, she'd become angry about their lack of progress. And then she worried about running out of time.

Something clicked in Sean's mind. Phil Meade must be the link. If they could come up with a motive for Richard's murder, then Rafe Neilson would launch a homicide investigation and presumably prove that Richard was murdered. Then Phil's attack on Ann would be meaningless. The timing didn't matter much unless...

...unless Phil Meade could do something to discredit Ann. But what would Phil have on Ann? Was there something in her past she wanted to keep hidden?

Sean knew in his gut that he'd guessed right. But that didn't cheer him. If anything, he felt let down that Ann chose not to trust him. He decided to call her on it.

"Ann, is there anything you need to tell me before we get back to Glory?" he asked.

"Not that I can think of," she replied, too quickly.

"You know the kind of thing I mean," he said, softly. "A deep, dark secret that Phil Meade might be holding over your head like the Sword of Damocles?"

Ann made a show of looking at the dashboard clock. "I'm hungry. I see a gas station down the road that has a mini-mart. Let's pick up some snacks."

Sean kept his eyes on the road and off Ann. She had

understood his question but ignored it. He parked in front of the mini-mart. Ann held her hand out. "I'll drive the rest of the way."

"You're under no obligation to tell me your secrets, Ann. But I'm trying to help you battle Phil Meade. I can't do that until you trust me completely."

"I do trust you, Sean." She stepped out of the car.

"But?"

"Leave it at that." He saw an emotion on her face that he hadn't yet seen: outright fear.

She's terrified about what Phil Meade might do. And she won't share her fears with me. How can I help her if she won't trust me—and if I haven't earned her trust by now, will I ever earn it?

NINE

Ann glanced at Sean asleep in the passenger seat and said, "Time to wake up."

He yawned and stretched. "Where are we?"

"Glory is around the next turn. I'll have you back at the Scottish Captain in five minutes."

"For some reason, I feel ready to spend the rest of the day in bed."

"I'm not surprised. You're still recovering from a nasty whack on the head."

He shrugged and made a loud *hmm*.

"I take your hum as agreement with my diagnosis," she said.

He made another *hmm*.

"I'm impressed. You do passable cat imitations."

"You've only heard my routine stuff. Prepare to be dazzled by my fabulous purr." He rolled the final *r-r-r* for more than ten seconds.

Ann laughed a bit. She appreciated his sense of humor and the fact that he was trying to cheer her up. She felt a twinge of guilt as she thought of the argument they'd just had, and the way she'd shut Sean out. But she didn't have to share her past with a man she had met four days ago, she thought. *There's no reason to tell him what happened seven years ago. Not now, not ever.*

"We've arrived," he said, as the tree-lined state road abruptly became Glory's Main Street in front of the town's garish sign. Its tall red and gold letters shouted, Welcome To Glory, North Carolina. We're Happy You're Here! Sean began to chuckle.

"I'll bite," she said. "What's so amusing about our welcome sign?"

"Well, the last time I saw that sign, a hurricane was bearing down on Glory. Carlo and I talked about adding 'Except for Gilda' to the bottom."

Ann trembled as the memory of that night seemed to fill her stomach with ice.

"I've made you upset again," Sean said, "I'm sorry. I'm sorry. I'm sorry. When will I learn to think before I open my mouth?"

"I'm not upset," she said.

"Your face says that you are. I seem to have a knack for saying stupid things that make you unhappy."

Ann didn't know how to respond. *And I have a knack for insulting you.* Anything she said would make the situation more uncomfortable for both of them. Fortunately, her cell phone broke the awkward silence with its loud rendition of "Stars and Stripes Forever." But this time, Sousa's familiar march seemed more ominous than rousing, and amplified the malevolent chill that had invaded Ann's spine.

"That's the ring tone that announces a call from Pastor Hartman," she said. "I'd better take it." She eased the Toyota into an empty parking spot on the south side of Main Street, and flipped open her phone.

"Hi, Daniel," she said.

"Ann, are you back in Glory?"

"Yep. I'm near the corner of Main and Broad."

"Come to the church as quickly as possible. We have a crisis here."

"What's wrong?"

"Phil Meade stomped into my office ten minutes ago and announced to me that he'd arranged a meeting to talk about you. At eleven this morning."

"A meeting about me? What kind of meeting? And why?"

"Those were my first two questions, but Phil wouldn't tell me anything more, other than that he'd invited as many members of the church's elder board as he could find in town this morning. And several other interested parties."

"I wonder how Phil defines 'interested party.'" Ann had an abrupt thought. "If this hastily called get-together is about me, how come Phil didn't send me an invitation?"

"That was the third question I asked him," Daniel said. "I told Phil that I'd put a stop to the entire meeting if you weren't present. He growled a bit, but finally agreed that I should summon you. Consider yourself summoned."

"Thank you, Daniel." She tried unsuccessfully to control the quiver she heard in her voice. "I guess that Phil is still riding his favorite hobby horse. He won't stop hounding me until he proves that I am completely responsible for Richard's death. Don't let Phil start complaining about me until I arrive."

Ann shut her phone and then maneuvered her car into the traffic lane.

"Where are we going?" Sean asked.

"To the Scottish Captain."

"Ann, come on. I couldn't help overhear your end of the conversation and you don't have to be a genius to understand that Phil Meade has set up some kind of kangaroo court, with you as the guest of honor."

Ann fought back tears. Sean's description of Phil's impromptu meeting was probably more accurate than she wanted to contemplate just then. She stared at the road.

"Phil Meade is a major pain in the patootie, but I can deal with him."

"Maybe. But *we* can deal with him a lot more effectively."

"Sean, this is all about me."

"Wrong, Ann. It's all about *us*. I was at the church the evening everything went bad. You keep forgetting that I urged you to call Richard Squires."

"Phil Meade is obsessed with me. He won't even recall your name."

"Stop wasting time. If you don't get to Glory Community quickly, your pastor will be forced to begin the meeting without you."

"Fine!" She made a sharp U-turn and hit the accelerator harder than she meant to. She pulled into the church's parking lot scarcely forty seconds later.

Ann slipped out of the car without speaking to Sean and strode toward the church's side entrance. She realized that Sean was following close behind.

"You're not going to attend this meeting," she said.

"Of course I am."

Ann stopped and faced Sean. "It's a five block walk to the Scottish Captain," she said firmly. "Turn left on Broad Street and keep going." Sean just stared at her.

She turned and flung open the heavy door. Daniel hadn't mentioned a location, but the meeting would probably be in the large classroom across from his office.

There were twelve people waiting for her in the classroom when she arrived. Daniel and Phil were perched on the teacher's desk in the front of the room. Five of Glory Community's seven elders sat together in a group on the left side of the room. A man and a woman who both looked vaguely familiar were sitting in front of Phil. Ann assumed they were connected with Glory's emergency command center and were at the meeting to support Phil.

Three other participants had taken seats on the right side of the room: Rafe Neilson, Rex Grainger, the editor of the *Glory Gazette,* and a heavyset man with a camera dangling from a lanyard around his neck.

Blast! Rex is here to do a story on me—and he brought a photographer to take pictures.

Ann didn't know where to sit. Daniel resolved her dilemma by pulling an empty chair to the left of the desk and angling it so that Ann could see Phil and everyone else who might choose to speak during the meeting.

Phil rose from his seat on the edge of the desk and cleared his throat. "Good morning, ladies and gentlemen, thank you all for coming."

"Excuse me, Mr. Meade," Daniel interrupted, preventing Phil from saying anything else. "Before we begin this meeting, I want to establish three ground rules. First—you invited us here today, but because the principal topic on the agenda is the performance of a church employee, I intend to act as moderator.

"Second—you apparently have something you wish to say to the elders of the church. This ad-hoc gathering will afford you the opportunity. However, this is not an official elder board meeting and none of us are here today to make decisions.

"Third—unless you object, I intend to open the proceedings with a prayer."

Ann saw Phil Meade's eyes grow wide. He glared at Daniel but seemed to decide that it made no sense to argue with a respected pastor, or object to an opening prayer. He gave a vague wave to signal his acquiescence.

"Heavenly Father," Daniel began, "we ask You to send Your Holy Spirit to be a participant with us today. Give us wisdom, good judgment and understanding. Let nothing be said in anger this afternoon, but rather let all of us who take the floor speak the truth in love. We ask these things in Jesus' name. Amen."

Ann spoke her amen, then noted that Phil was gazing intently at her. She shivered at his cheerfully confident expression—then had a spark of insight.

He knows about me. He found out what no one else in Glory knows. That's why he looks so pleased with himself—he's going to tell everyone, and he can hardly wait to begin, she thought.

God, why are You putting me in the spotlight again? Didn't I have enough pain seven years ago?

Ann heaved a sigh as another brief quiver of fear gave way to a curious feeling of relief. *Okay, let it all come out. I'm tired of worrying about ancient history. Whatever happens today, happens.*

Phil moved to the open space in front of the desk. "Once again, ladies and gentlemen, I thank you for honoring my request to speak to you."

Phil paused for a moment and used the time to smile at his audience. Ann noted that most of the people in the classroom smiled back. The two exceptions were Daniel and Rafe. Well, at least she knew who her friends were today.

"As I explained when I invited you, I want to talk about Ann Trask. Specifically, her actions on the evening that

Gilda passed close to Glory." Another short pause. "I am well aware that some of you don't agree with my assertion that Miss Trask committed a significant error in judgment that led directly to the unnecessary death of Richard Squires."

He took a deep breath then resumed talking. "Let me assure you that I am not obsessed with the need to make a point or have my opinions vindicated. What disturbs me most is that Miss Trask fully understands what she did wrong on Monday evening, but she refuses to admit her mistake—or accept responsibility."

Ann scanned the "interested parties" Phil had invited. Rex Grainger was furiously typing on his laptop, while his photographer was surreptitiously snapping photos without using a flash.

"Glory may only be a small town," Phil said, "but everyone who takes responsibility for public safety needs to scrupulously honest, both with themselves, and with their colleagues."

Ann glanced at Rafe, then Daniel. Both seem puzzled by Phil's comment, but she knew exactly what he meant. Here it comes: Camp Carolina Pines.

Phil unfolded a sheet of paper and studied it briefly. "It pains me to report that Miss Trask's decision to call Richard Squires to Glory Community Church is not her first life-threatening error in judgment. What she did the other evening is consistent with her behavior in the past— a past, incidentally, that she has kept secret from all of us."

Ann had her eyes fixed on the vinyl-tiled floor in front of her chair, but she heard several murmurs from the elders in the room.

"Seven years ago," Phil said, "after completing her sophomore year at college, Miss Trask served as a camp counselor at Camp Carolina Pines. She had held the same job the previous summer.

"Late on the afternoon of July 26, a severe thunderstorm struck the campgrounds with high winds, heavy rains and large chunks of hail."

Ann stared harder at the floor. She couldn't stop her mind from replaying those terrible few minutes. The gray sky had grown dark as twilight. The hail had looked more like chunks of steel than ice, and the ten girls in her care—all between seven and ten—had begun to scream.

Phil went on. "There was an old, unused shed on the campgrounds—a structure off-limits to all staff and campers, because everyone in leadership considered it unsafe. On her own initiative, Miss Trask led the ten children into the shed, ostensibly to escape the storm. Within minutes, a gust of wind collapsed the shed, trapping everyone beneath the wreckage. Frantic searchers did not find Miss Trask and the children until close to midnight."

Ann would never forget the noise of the wind and the total darkness. They'd been trapped under the shed's fallen roof, with the wind shrieking outside and the kids alternately crying and screaming.

Phil continued. "As a direct result of Miss Trask's poor judgment, six of the children she led into the condemned shed were injured, two of them critically. Blessedly, those children eventually recovered. However, their parents charged Miss Trask with negligence and filed a civil lawsuit against the camp. True to form, Miss Trask insisted that she had made the right decision at the time. The suit was eventually settled. Miss Trask never worked at the camp again.

"I can understand why Miss Trask withheld details of Camp Carolina Pines when she applied for her post at

Glory Community Church. The past is the best predictor of the future. Wise elders might well have become concerned by Miss Trask's failure to follow orders and her refusal to accept responsibility for her actions."

Ann looked around the room. The elders seemed perplexed by Phil Meade's revelation. Rafe looked confused and even Daniel appeared bewildered.

I hope I didn't lose the most important support I had.

A loud bang startled Ann. Someone had flung open the classroom door with enough force to make the wall shake. A loud voice followed the unexpected noise.

"My name is Sean Miller and I have something important to say."

Ann grimaced. Why hadn't Sean listened to her and stayed away from the meeting? Anything he said now was bound to throw fuel on the fire.

Not that it makes much difference. People can't think less of me than they do right now.

"Leave this room immediately, Mr. Miller," Phil Meade shouted, "or I will have you thrown out!"

Sean marched toward the desk and pointed his right index finger directly at Phil's nose. "You may succeed in bullying others, Mr. Meade, but all I see is a pretentious local official who has chosen to wield his authority in an abusive manner." Sean took a breath. "I've dealt with your kind before. You don't frighten me, sir."

Sean could almost feel the anger radiating from Phil's glower.

"Our purpose here is not to frighten anyone," Daniel said, "but this is not an open meeting, Mr. Miller. All of the attendees are here this morning because they were invited by Mr. Meade or by me."

Sean willed himself to speak softly and evenly. "I know that, and I apologize for my dramatic entrance—and for eavesdropping," he said, looking directly at Ann. She met his gaze only for a moment, but it was long enough for Sean to see the pain in her eyes.

"In point of fact, I should have been invited to this meeting, because I have important information about the circumstances leading up to the death of Richard Squires. Simply put, I played a major role in Ann Trask's decision to call Mr. Squires to Glory Community Church to repair the failed generator. If you fault her for bringing him to the church, you must also fault me."

"Poppycock!" Phil said. "I threw this northern carpet-bagger out of my office two days ago. He's a know-nothing. Ann Trask enlisted him to muddy the waters."

Sean replied, "Even you can't be dumb enough to believe something that nonsensical."

"Stop right there!" Daniel shouted. "Both of you! I won't tolerate any more personal insults." He pointed a finger at Sean. "Mr. Miller, I will give you exactly three minutes to share your information. After that, I will throw you out of this room myself, if necessary. Understood?"

Sean nodded. "Yes, sir." He suddenly wished he'd that worn his bright red Storm Channel jacket. A "power color" would help focus the participants' attention on him. Well, he'd have to pull them in with a firm voice, commanding body language and strong gestures.

Praise the Lord I paid attention to Carlo Vaughn on his good days.

"Ladies and gentlemen," he began. "As some of you know, I work for the Storm Channel. On the evening that Gilda came to Glory, I received permission from Miss Trask to park the broadcast van in the church's parking lot.

Miss Trask was a gracious hostess. She invited the Storm Channel weather reporter and me to take shelter inside the church after our broadcasts were over.

"When Miss Trask learned that I operated the diesel generator inside our broadcast van, she requested that I check the operational status of the church's emergency generator. The generator stopped running a few seconds after I started the diesel engine. The signal light indicated a problem in the fuel system. Miss Trask asked if I could do anything to fix the problem. Alas, I had to refuse to because we were about to go on the air with a live broadcast. I called her attention to the note that Richard Squires had posted on the wall. The instructions were short and specific—'In case of a problem with the generator, call Richard Squires.' I urged her to make the call. From my perspective, she did exactly what was prudent and necessary.

"If I'd ignored my responsibility to the Storm Channel and had taken time to work on the diesel engine, Richard Squires would probably be alive today." Sean glanced at Phil Meade. "So why not say that I'm responsible for his death?"

"More poppycock!" Phil said.

Sean decided not to exchange any more verbal blows with Phil Meade. He'd made his point. He thanked them for listening and moved quickly toward the door. It wasn't until he was outside in the corridor that he realized Ann had followed him.

He braced himself for her fury, but she surprised him with a smile. "Thanks for trying to help, Sean, but you aren't responsible for Richard Squires' death because you didn't demand to be given a position of responsibility despite the concerns of several people. I did. Phil Meade didn't want me to be in charge of the emergency shelter, but I insisted. He'll never get over that I challenged his judgment, and won. And now he's using my checkered past to prove he was right, and I was wrong."

Sean took Ann's arm and led her to a sofa positioned near the narthex's back wall. "*What* checkered past, Ann? You were an eighteen-year-old kid trying to protect a group of campers from a bad thunderstorm. A falling-down shed might have been a poor choice, but what was your alternative? Stay out of the open and get clobbered by hail? Or shelter under trees and possibly get hit by lightning?"

He looked closely at her and could see the exhaustion on her pretty face. "Decisions you made back then have absolutely nothing to do with what happened the other night. Apparently, Phil doesn't know much about the concept of relevance."

Ann shrugged. "But he is right about one thing. I panicked that evening. I didn't want to be alone in the dark with the wind blowing outside. I spent almost seven hours trapped under that collapsed roof, unable to help the kids or myself. I still have nightmares about that night. I'd rather die than repeat the experience."

Sean put his hand over hers. He half expected her to pull away, but she didn't. Her hand felt warm and soft under his. "That's a nasty memory to cope with. No wonder you don't like to talk about Camp Carolina Pines."

Ann squeezed his fingers tightly and turned in her seat to face him. The pain was still there, but holding his hand seemed to give her comfort.

"Now everyone thinks I lied to the church, and I have only myself to blame. I should have mentioned the camp, but I convinced myself that most people knew about it. After all, it was no secret. Newspapers and TV stations all over the state covered the story."

Sean studied her face. He could see tears in her eyes, but she seemed relieved—relieved to have finally unburdened herself of her secret. She looked up at him, and his heart nearly stopped in his chest. He was having trouble focusing on her words.

"I wish the lawsuit had come to trial," she was saying. "If it had, I'd have been able to tell my side of the story. But because the camp settled, there's still a big cloud over my head. Anyway, for better or worse, the accident changed my career path. I'd intended to be a teacher, but I was so shaken that I didn't want to work with kids anymore. I went back to college two years later and majored in business administration." She paused for a moment, then said, "Sean, I'm sorry. I'm sorry I wasn't able to tell you my secret."

Without thinking, Sean put his hands on her shoulders and turned her to face him. He leaned forward and gently brushed his lips against hers. He heard her gasp, but she didn't pull away for several seconds. He felt fairly sure that she kissed him back.

When she spoke, she asked, "Why did you do that?"

"I wanted to. And I couldn't think of any other way to make you stop beating yourself up."

She grinned. "So if I continue to beat myself up, does that mean you'll kiss me again?"

Sean smiled. "Again and again."

Ann laughed and Sean reached out and drew her toward him.

TEN

"You probably shouldn't kiss the church administrator in the narthex," Ann said.

"Is that one of Glory Community's bylaws?" he asked, grinning impishly.

She fought not to laugh as she stood up. "Kissing is simply not done in the narthex."

"I'm confused. I distinctly remember that you kissed me back—in the narthex."

"A gentleman would not have remembered. You are incorrigible! Now let's get out of here before Phil Meade and the others finish the meeting."

"Good idea. If they catch us kissing, it could lessen the strength of our case," he said as he leaned in to kiss her again.

Ann dodged his kiss and took his hand, leading him to the front door. "Let's walk," she said. Sean pushed the door open and they walked down the front path toward Oliver Street.

She felt like a different person—joyful and at ease and pleased to know that Sean was only inches away. A switch inside her had flipped. Something enduring had begun to gel. She couldn't stop caring for Sean even if she wanted to at this point.

She realized that Sean had a remarkable ability to change her perception of the world. She'd left the meeting feeling hollow, defeated. But Sean's sweet kisses had banished her pessimism and transformed her vision of the future from negative to positive. He'd even managed to push the practical aspects of their relationship from her mind. Somehow, it no longer mattered to her that he lived hundreds of miles away, or that he planned to leave Glory in two days.

"It's nice to see you happy again," Sean said. He playfully swung her arm. Could this be what romance feels like? she mused. Romance! The very notion startled her.

Ann had never thought herself romantic, but rather a loner, a woman who intentionally shied away from romantic entanglements. After all, if she became involved with a man, she'd have to tell him about her past—share her deepest secrets, shock him with the details of her failures.

But Sean hadn't been shocked. He had learned the worst about her and taken it in stride. Perhaps even more surprising, he seemed to understand the pain she felt. But he didn't seem to understand her way of coping with it.

"Sean, something you said in the narthex—you told me that your kiss stopped me from beating myself up."

Sean tugged on her hand so that she'd stop and face him. "That incident at Camp Carolina Pines happened seven years ago."

She couldn't help frowning. "I loathe that word. The lawyers called what occurred at the camp an 'incident.' It's so impersonal, so disconnected from me. I prefer 'accident' or 'mistake.'"

Sean was no longer smiling at her. "Seven years is a long time, but you still have nightmares about it. You've probably thought about it every day, squandering untold emotional energy keeping your past hidden from the people around you, and every chance you get, you blame yourself for what happened to those kids."

"You make it sound like I have a choice."

"Don't you?" He began to sing. "'O what peace we often forfeit, O what needless pain we bear/All because we do not carry everything to God in prayer.'"

"You can sing!" she exclaimed. He laughed. She said, "That's from 'What a Friend We Have in Jesus.'"

"It's my favorite line from my favorite hymn," Sean said. "You ought to pay attention to the words when the choir sings them."

She could almost feel his gaze searching her face.

"Ann, you strike me as a wholly committed Christian in every possible way except one. You refuse to turn your problems over to God. You doggedly try to solve them yourself, including the biggest challenge you live with— how to get out from under an accident that changed your life seven years ago."

Ann dropped his hand and took a step backward. "And you strike me as an equally committed Christian, except for one thing. You have a propensity to judge your fellow believers."

"Touché." He held up his hands in a gesture of surrender. "Guilty as charged."

She decided not to tell Sean that she'd heard a dozen different ministers, including Daniel, preach on the importance of turning the challenges in her life over to God. But weren't there limits? Why should she expect Him to undo the mess at Camp Carolina Pines? Shifting the burden of her mistake to God would be a total cop-out.

Sean seemed to guess her thoughts. "Remember what

Paul said. 'Do not be anxious about anything, but in everything, by prayer and petition, with thanksgiving, present your requests to God. And the peace of God, which transcends all understanding, will guard your hearts and your minds in Christ Jesus.'"

"I know how Christianity works." She was angry—Sean's zealous pushing and prodding was getting to her. "You don't have to tell me to 'let go and let God.' Last winter I bought a thousand bumper stickers for members with that phrase in inch-high letters."

"Apparently you didn't pay much attention to the words." Sean brought his face close to hers. "I suspect that God's been encouraging you to let go for lots of years. But you're too stubborn—you like to do things your own way."

"That sounds remarkably like another judgment, Sean."

"I hate to see you suffering needless pain. I can't help it—not since you returned my kiss in the narthex, and violated a dozen or two church rules. The thing is—and it took me years to figure this out—God can't use you fully for his purposes until you're willing to let go completely."

"If you put a sock in your lecture, I promise to ponder everything you said."

"No need to make promises—I intend to remind you, unmercifully," Sean said, smiling.

They ambled east on Oliver Street without talking. When they reached Snacks of Glory, Ann studied their reflections in the plate-glass window and decided that they looked "right" together, like a man and a woman who'd known each other far longer than three and a half days. Sean was holding her hand again, although she couldn't recall when or where on their silent journey he had reached for her.

Ann looked at Sean and saw his attention focused on

the park across the street. "Those are two bronze statues there—why are they both wearing dresses?"

"Those are kilts, you knucklehead. Duncan and Moira McGregor led the group of Scots who founded Glory in 1733. If you browse through Founder's Park, you'll find a lovely copse in the middle that houses their grave sites."

He chuckled. "I stand corrected. Another piece of Glory charm."

"I'm thrilled that Glory amuses your wee brain."

"It does! In fact, perhaps I should take a picture for posterity. Why don't you stand in front of that neon SOGgy Burger for me."

Sean held his cell phone up and took a photo of Ann standing beneath the SOGgy Burger.

"What do you intend to do with that photo?"

He smiled at her and she felt a sudden stab of sadness, thinking of him looking at the photo when he arrived in New York several days from now. She pushed the thought away and strode ahead, confident that Sean would catch up quickly. They turned south when they arrived at Front Street. The piles of debris they'd seen yesterday had been hauled away. She paused to study the Albemarle Sound. The afternoon sun streaming over her shoulder made the water sparkle. Two small sailboats zipped along the beautifully serene surface, propelled by the cool breeze.

"What a difference a day makes," Ann said. "We'll soon forget that Gilda paid us a visit. All except Phil Meade—and me."

They came to a grassy strip and passed a couple playing Frisbee fetch with their golden retriever, who seemed inordinately delighted by the game. The smiling retriever loped over to Sean for a behind-the-ear scratch.

"Phil Meade's the opposite of a golden retriever," Sean

said. "He's a stubborn bulldog who won't let go of the bone in his mouth."

Ann shook her head. "Don't insult a noble canine breed. Phil is a junkyard mongrel—one of the really nasty ones."

Sean sat down on a bench. Ann sat beside him. "Where do we go from here?" he asked.

She hadn't expected Sean to ask the question that was at the top of her mind, and she labored to come up with a sensible reply. "I don't have an answer. I suppose that our future will depend on your career and what you plan to do."

Sean beamed at her. "That's not what I meant, although that's the nicest thing you've ever said to me. You think that we could have a future together."

Ann looked away, sure that every inch of her skin was red with embarrassment. Sean came to her rescue and changed the subject.

"I meant where we can go from here to find a motive for murder. Encouraging Rafe to find the person who killed Richard remains the best—and maybe only—way to convince Phil that he's wrong about you."

Ann heard herself sigh. "I may sound like a broken iPod, but I'm not surprised that we can't turn up a motive. Richard was too nice a person to make enemies."

"Let's go with that," Sean said. "Niceness eliminates motives related to jealousy, fear and revenge—but it leaves money on the table. Money is always a potential motive for murder."

"Richard's chief asset was Squires' Place." She made a face. "We visited his restaurant and learned about Hayden, but that's all we learned."

"We didn't prod very hard. In fact, Sheila Parker told us very little. I say we try again. How about right now?"

Ann couldn't think of a reason to disagree, other than

that Sheila might not want to talk about Richard again. And even if she agreed—well, Sean might fancy himself a detective, but he didn't have the streak of ferocity that encouraged witnesses to spill their guts, so to speak.

Thank goodness! I wouldn't care for him if he did.

Sean murmured a short prayer. "Thank You, Lord, for what we've learned to date about Richard Squires, but we need to make more progress—quickly." He'd seen discouragement explode on Ann's face, her reluctant acceptance of defeat. Now that Phil Meade had done his worst, she'd seemed to have lost much of her motivation to press on. Another disappointment or two and she might call an end to their investigation. Then she'd spend the rest of her life brooding about the *two* mistakes she'd made.

I won't let that happen. No matter what.

He hadn't told Ann, but time had become his enemy, too. Late September was the height of the hurricane season. A new tropical depression could be forming right now in the eastern Atlantic Ocean. In a handful of days it could swell into a named hurricane zooming toward the United States. When that happened, his sojourn in Glory would end with a frantic telephone call from Cathy McCabe. She wouldn't care that his heart wasn't in weather reporting this week, or that he'd made promises to an amazing local gal. Cathy would give him a new assignment and expect him to take it—or else.

They walked directly to the alley off Campbell Street.

"Do you think Sheila's at Squires' Place?" he asked.

"That's where I'd be. If she plans to open the restaurant on Saturday night, there's a mountain of work to do." Ann dug in her purse for a mirror. "Yikes. I look like a train wreck. Too many tears, too much wind. You should have told me."

Sean shrugged. "You look great to me. Who cares about smudged makeup?"

"First Carlo, now you. Storm Channel men must get advanced training in lying to women." She delved into her bag again. "You don't have to supervise my repair efforts. Ring the bell."

The steel door swung open. Sheila's unhappy face came into view. "You're back."

"We have a few additional questions to ask about Richard," Sean said. "We'll be brief."

"I hope so. I'm very busy today."

They followed Sheila directly to Richard's office, sitting on the same sofa as the day before. Sheila perched on the edge of Richard's desk. Her expression made Sean think of a bird of prey—small cold eyes filled with unwavering purpose, staring eagerly at lunch. What, he wondered, had happened since they saw her last? And what had Richard Squires seen in this woman? "Okay," she snapped, "ask your questions."

Sean saw Ann staring at the desk, looking surprised. Only then, did he notice that he could see the polished walnut desktop. No more piles of paper. For some unknown reason, Sheila had taken time from her allegedly busy schedule to tidy Richard's office.

"I see that you organized Richard's paperwork," he said.

"I filed everything. I had to. Richard's children asked me to run the restaurant while it's still a restaurant."

It was an odd remark, but Sean understood what she meant. Richard's kids had promoted Sheila from hostess to manager.

She went on, "Richard could run Squires' Place surrounded by disorder, I can't."

"It sounds to me that Richard's children plan to move

ahead with the development project you told us about yesterday, the one involving Mr. Hayden, in Norfolk."

"Of course they do!" She looked at Sean with disbelief. "Wouldn't you? It's a fabulous opportunity. The demolition will begin in November."

Sean thought for a moment. She must've gotten that tidbit of information from Richard's children, but where did they get it? Certainly not from Miles Hayden. The new project couldn't begin until after the details of Richard's will had been settled. Hayden knew that; he wouldn't be foolish enough to promise a specific start date so early in the probate process.

Maybe the date wasn't a promise but a speculation made to a big-mouthed, big-haired friend who wasn't good at keeping secrets?

Did Sheila know Hayden? She might have met him during one of Hayden's visits to Glory to explain his development plan to Richard. Had she kept in touch with Hayden to…uh, broaden her opportunities? Was she one of the "several friends" in Glory that Hayden had mentioned?

Sean stopped his ruminating when he noted that Ann's eyes had become bright, all but merry. He'd seen that look before, Sean thought. She was going to skewer Sheila.

"Let me be the first to congratulate you, Sheila," Ann said. "Managing Squires' Place is an enormous responsibility. Richard's children have given you a tremendous vote of confidence."

"Thank you. With God's help, I'll do a good job."

"I'm certain you will, which leads me to ask a question. Where did you learn to run a large restaurant? People don't realize how complex a task it can be, what with planning menus, buying food, supervising the cook and wait staffs, taking care of the finances, dealing with daily problems, chatting up customers—the list goes on and on. Doing a thorough job can take sixteen hours a day."

"Indeed it can. I've done it all."

"Now, that's what baffles me. I've always thought of hostesses as the Vanna Whites of the restaurant biz. You smile prettily, walk people to their tables and hand out menus. Hardly the right training for managing Squires' Place."

Sheila's expression darkened. All pretense at civility vanished. She crossed her arms and glared at Ann.

"That's a stupid thing to say, Miss Trask—even if you believe it's true—but I don't think that you are a stupid woman. Well, neither am I. I can think of only one explanation for your insults. You're baiting me. You hope that I'll overreact to your absurd claims and say something foolish."

Sheila stood up and moved closer to Sean. "What is this all about? Why do you want information about Richard and his restaurant? And don't tell me it has to do with planning Richard's funeral. I gave you that opening yesterday, but it's no longer available. All the planning's been done."

Sean sucked in a mouthful of air then said, "We're trying to understand all that we can about Richard Squires."

"Why?"

"We have our reasons." Sean knew it was an inane thing to say the instant the words left his lips.

Sheila picked up the telephone.

"Get out of here," she said. "You're trespassing on private property. I'll call the police if you don't leave immediately."

Sean knew that he'd have to tell Sheila at least part of the truth. He had no other choice. "Okay, I'll answer your question, but you might want to sit down first." When Sheila made no move to sit, Sean continued. "There's a strong possibility that Richard's death wasn't an accident."

Sheila took a step forward, halting only when her face was inches from his. He could feel her breath on his cheek.

"What a dreadful, hurtful thing to say. A church steeple fell on Richard. How can that be anything but an accident?"

Sheila backed away from Sean and turned her anger on Ann.

"This is all your doing," she said. "I've heard people in Glory talk about you. They say you're responsible for Richard's death because you called him to the church to fix the generator. Now you're trying to put the blame on someone else."

"If that's true," Ann said, "why are you afraid of me?"

"I'm not afraid of you."

"But you are. I hear fear in your voice."

Sean stared at Sheila with newfound interest. He realized that Ann was right; Sheila's bluster had been full of fear. He decided to push her further.

"I'm quite serious, Sheila—do you mind if I call you Sheila?" He didn't wait for an answer. "The police are aware of several suspicious factors associated with Richard's death."

Her eyes opened wide. "What kind of suspicious factors?"

"On the night that Richard died, he parked his car toward the rear of the church parking lot. Yet when he left the church, he walked in a different direction, during torrential rain. There wasn't any reason for him to be in the location where the steeple fell."

"But…" Sheila seemed lost in thought, deliberating mightily about what Sean had revealed. She finally said, "I might have an explanation for that."

"What explanation?" he said softly, barely able to control his incredulity.

Sheila clasped her hands together. "Richard called me from the church after he finished fixing the generator. He was unhappy. He said that someone had sabotaged it."

Sean heard Ann gasp as she leaped to her feet.

"He told you someone had intentionally disabled our generator?"

"Yes," Sheila said. "Perhaps that's why he didn't walk directly toward his car. Maybe he planned to stay at the church a while longer?"

"Why didn't you tell that to the police?" Ann asked Sheila.

"No one has asked me about that night. And anyway, the newspaper said that Richard had been killed in a freak accident. I didn't think what Richard told me made any difference. I still don't." She grimaced. "No more questions today. I've got lots to do," Shelia said, glancing at her watch, "and this conversation is going nowhere."

Sean grasped Ann's hand and moved toward the door.

"Thank you for your time," he said. He could tell Ann wasn't ready to leave, but it was clear to him that they'd learn nothing more from Sheila today.

Sean and Ann walked to Glory Community Church side by side, talking about sabotage. "What could it mean?" she asked.

"It means that someone wanted Richard to be at the church that evening. Someone who intended to kill him and wanted to hide behind Gilda."

"But we still don't have a motive."

"Not quite, but we've made a genuine chunk of progress," Sean said.

"Should we tell Rafe?"

"Not yet. Sheila didn't mention the call until after I'd told her the death was suspicious. Rafe will want more than hearsay evidence."

"Onward goes the investigation," she said, almost gleefully.

For the first time since they began this investigation, he could see hope in Ann's lovely face.

Praise the Lord.

ELEVEN

If Ann had been able to squeeze beneath the cushions of Daniel's leather sofa, she would have tried to disappear from sight. She'd never felt more wretched, more humiliated in all her life.

Daniel was standing next to the sofa, Ann's small hand sandwiched between his large hands.

"I'm sorry that I had to be the one to tell you," he said, "but I wanted to be sure you knew before the word trickled throughout Glory and you heard about it from someone else."

She nodded, sniffed, then nodded again. "Thank you, Daniel. I'm really not surprised. Even though Phil Meade isn't a member of the church, he's a respected person in Glory. People listen to what he has to say."

"Not this time. Our elders are intelligent people. Once they understand what's driving Phil—a single-minded commitment to pay you back for perceived slights—they'll reject his accusations."

Ann forced a smile. They both knew that Daniel had put a hopeful face on a hopeless state of affairs. She owed Daniel her best efforts to control her tattered emotions. The sobbing could wait until later, when she was alone.

"Would you like a cup of tea?" he asked.

Ann cleared her throat, then said, "I'd love some."

"I'll be right back."

"No need to rush." Ann noticed that Daniel seemed delighted with even a brief opportunity to leave his office. None of this was his doing and he must hate every miserable aspect of the situation. She could only imagine his reaction when he'd opened the letter first thing this morning.

The elders had held a private meeting on Thursday evening. They hadn't invited Daniel, but they had invited Phil Meade. They'd taken a vote, summarized their conclusions in a brief letter and slipped the letter under Daniel's door.

Dear Pastor Hartman,

The three members of the Elder Board whose signatures you will find below were shocked and dismayed to learn that Miss Ann Trask, the recently hired administrator of Glory Community Church, did not reveal the details of her "incident" at Camp Carolina Pines, some seven years ago.

We reluctantly interpret Miss Trask's decision to withhold important information as an indication of her dishonesty. We have lost confidence in her judgment and her truthfulness. Consequently, we have begun to doubt her explanation of the chain of events that led to the tragic death of Mr. Richard Squires.

We urge you to appoint a special committee of church members to examine every aspect of Miss Trask's behavior during the time the emergency shelter was open. We especially seek clarification about the necessity of summoning Mr. Squires to repair the church's generator during the height of Hurricane Gilda.

Daniel returned with a tall ceramic mug and sat next to her on the sofa. She sensed that he'd cranked his bedside manner up to maximum tranquility while brewing her tea.

"You know," he said calmly, "that the circumstances are far less bleak than you may think they are. The three elders who signed the letter represent a minority of the elder board. That means that the majority of elders and me— remember, I have a vote on the board—have confidence in you. You'll weather this storm as successfully as Glory weathered Gilda."

Ann glanced at Daniel and struggled mightily to hold back her tears. "Thank you for your kindness, Daniel, but we both know that I have to end this mess now. A battle inside the elder board will spill over into the congregation and hurt the church. Glory Community has had more than its share of conflicts recently. Our members don't need a new war over me."

"I don't want you to leave, Ann. You're my friend, and the best church administrator I've ever worked with."

"I don't want to leave, Daniel, but I have to. There's no alternative. Phil Meade will keep stirring the pot until I'm gone." She gave a pained smile. "And the fact is that much of what he thinks about me is true. One of the reasons I wanted to stay in the church during the hurricane was to prove to the world—but mostly to me—that I could handle an emergency. All I proved, though, is that I don't have what it takes to manage a tough situation."

"That's baloney. You're an excellent manager."

"I won't lie to myself anymore, Daniel, or to you. I

counted on this job to erase my past. I know now that was foolish of me. My present and my past have conspired against me. Maybe I have to accept the possibility that Richard Squires's death is my fault. I called him to the church. If I hadn't made that call—well, who knows what might've happened?"

"Please reconsider," Daniel said simply.

"There's nothing for me to reconsider. I'm tired of brawling with Phil Meade, and I'm tired of pretending there's a light at the end of the tunnel. All I can do is start over again, somewhere else."

"How can I give you up without a fight?"

She leaned forward and kissed his forehead.

"I love you, Reverend Daniel Hartman. I'll miss you most of all when I leave Glory." She stood up. "Now let me get out of here before I flood your office with salt water."

"You can't leave, Ann," Sean said. "I won't let you. Not when we're so close to finding a logical motive."

Sean reached for her hand; she pulled lose from his grip and climbed the remaining steps to her front porch. "It won't make any difference if you do find the reason that Richard was murdered. Half of the church's elders don't trust me anymore. I can't work in a church led by people who've written me off. There are no other options for me. I have to leave Glory Community Church, and I have to leave Glory."

"Rafe's homicide investigation will spin the elders around. Their minds will change once they learn that Richard wasn't killed by a freak accident."

"Rafe's investigation is a pipe dream," she said. "Nothing but a fantasy—a trip to cloud-cuckoo-land we enjoyed for a day or two. The time has come to get real. You said it yesterday. Rafe needs compelling evidence to move ahead, and we don't have any."

"I'm still looking."

"Please stop." She spoke with a commanding tone that broke his train of thought. He gave a small nod of submission.

She went on, "I gave Daniel my notice and I spoke to my mother. We haven't talked about where we might move when she sells this house, but I'll drive to Asheville on Monday and take a few days to figure things out."

"On Monday? Why the rush?"

"As I told Daniel, hanging around Glory for a week or two will give church members a chance to take sides and could trigger the kind of battle royal that I'm determined to prevent."

He moved close to her on the porch. "What about us, Ann? With all your talk of leaving, you haven't mentioned us. Are you also planning to leave me?"

She hesitated long enough to take a deep breath. "You have a great future ahead of you, Sean. I'd be a liability. Sean Miller, crack meteorologist, doesn't need deadweight trailing behind to slow him down." She took several steps back, away from him. "I'll say goodbye to you now, Sean. It will hurt us both needlessly if we see each other again." She held up a hand. "Please don't say anything that will make what I have to do more difficult. This is hard enough for me as it is."

All he could do for several seconds was stare at Ann.

He finally said, "You sound like you've thought this through."

"I have. Completely."

"Seven days ago, I might have simply let you go. But

that's not going to happen this week. Take a good look into my eyes, Ann. You'll see pain, but also obstinacy."

Ann stepped into her house and closed the door quietly, leaving Sean alone on her porch.

I've become as pigheaded as you, Ann Trask. I'll do whatever it takes to keep you in Glory.

Sean jogged back to the Scottish Captain, his mind working at a furious pace. He'd been on the verge of telling Ann that he loved her. One part of him wished that he had, but the other, more astute, part was glad that he hadn't. She'd convinced herself that she'd made the right decision. His profession of love would simply have made the situation worse. No. He'd save the talk of love for a better time. The right time. He wouldn't talk about his investigation anymore, either, but no way would he stop as she'd asked him to. Just the opposite. He would accelerate his search for the motive. And he would bring in the big guns to help.

He loped up the carpeted stairs to his room, sprawled on the bed and fired up his cell phone.

"Hi, Cathy, it's Sean."

"Howdy stranger. Do you still work for the Storm Channel?"

"Devotedly. I plan to pick up our broadcast van this afternoon."

"When will we see you in Long Island?"

"Actually, that's why I'm calling. Unless a storm pops up in the Atlantic, I'd like to use a few days of my vacation." He added, "I'm still feeling a bit shaky from the accident."

"We both know that field producers don't have feelings, but enjoy yourself with Miss What's-her-name. I picked Carlo up at the airport this morning. He claims that a domineering, utterly unladylike Southern gal has worked her wiles on you."

"Carlo is a numbskull."

"Yes, but his ratings are fabulous." She laughed. "Keep in touch."

"Hey! Before you hang up, will you transfer me to Mimi Gallagher?"

"Pardon me! Did I hear you right?"

"Believe it or not, I need a favor from her."

"Watch your wallet."

His line went quiet for a few seconds, and then he heard Mimi.

"This is Mimi Gallagher. Lucky you!"

"Mimi, it's Sean Miller. I'm calling from Glory, North Carolina."

"I didn't know that our masters had punished you. When will they let you return to civilization?"

"Glory is a delightful little town. Even you would enjoy living here."

"Wash your mouth out with soap immediately."

"Mimi, I need a favor."

"Wow! You must be desperate. I know what you straight arrows on the Storm Channel think about our enchanting Scandal Channel."

"You're right, I am desperate. I need your help—quickly."

"Okay, tell Mother Mimi what's wrong."

Sean chuckled. Mimi *was* old enough to be his mother, although few people would guess her chronological age. She had flame-red hair, genuine green eyes, pretty features and a lovely complexion—a winning combination wrought by her Irish father and French mother.

"When Gilda passed over Glory the other evening," Sean said, "a local man was killed."

"I heard about that. A church steeple fell on him in a parking lot. How very Wizard of Oz! I understand he was wearing ruby boots instead of ruby slippers."

"His name was Richard Squires, a local restaurateur who was loved by almost everyone."

"Almost?"

"He had at least one enemy. I'm pretty sure his death wasn't an accident. He went to the church to fix an emergency generator. After he fixed it, somebody clobbered him and placed his body under the steeple's wreckage. We have some evidence that the generator was sabotaged, a ploy to get Richard to the church that evening."

"How sure are you that the man was murdered?"

"Completely sure, except I can't find a motive. Squires apparently lived a perfect life and had no enemies," Sean said.

"So you called me?"

"I need to know how to conduct an effective investigation, ASAP."

The line went quiet—Mimi was thinking. "Here's the deal," she finally said. "I teach you how to interrogate your fellow man, and you give me the story when you complete your investigation."

"Why would you want the story? It hardly seems grist for the Scandal Channel's mill."

"Are you bonkers? Look at the elements. Beloved churchgoer. Wicked murderer. Treacherous steeple. Curious field producer. Sabotaged generator. All in a charming Southern town seething below the surface with tumultuous and deadly passions. I ask you—what more could we want?"

"I accept your offer."

"Not so fast." Mimi paused for a moment then said,

"Why are you, an unabashed civilian, involving yourself in a murder investigation? You have no reason to stick your nose where it doesn't belong. Curiosity isn't motivation enough."

"Well, everyone else in Glory is treating the incident as an accident."

"Maybe everyone else is right?"

"They aren't. But I *do* have a reason to get involved."

"I'm listening."

"Her name is Ann Trask. The town blowhard, a pinhead named Phil Meade, blames her for summoning Richard Squires to the church—"

"Where he got whomped by the steeple."

"Meade's giving her a hard time. He dug up some old dirt on Ann. She was involved in another bizarre accident seven years ago," Sean explained.

"The plot thickens."

"It does, but what happened seven years ago has nothing to do with the other night. Meade will have to back off when I help to prove that Richard Squires was murdered."

"I take it that Ann is the ill-mannered Southern lady Carlo mentioned to Cathy?"

"Consider the source."

Mimi laughed. "It's so much fun to watch young love wreak havoc on nice guys like you."

"Will you help me?"

"How could I not? Your almost-lady-friend will make my story even more appealing. 'Valiant field producer for the Storm Channel helps Carolinian lady in distress and lands the Gilda Ghoul.' That's a nifty name for a hurricane murderer, if I say so myself."

"Nifty and natty. What do I do first?"

"You buy a digital recorder small enough to hide in your

shirt pocket. Then you won't have to take notes, which puts some people off."

"Isn't hiding an electronic recorder cheating?"

"I do it all the time, but if it really bothers you, ask for permission to record conversations. Most folks will say yes if you tell them you have a rotten memory and will forget whatever they tell you."

"Who am I going to talk to?"

"People who knew Richard Squires well enough to be interested in his life," Mimi explained.

"Won't they ask me why I want to interview them?"

"Of course they will, which is why you need a good cover story."

"I'm a bad liar."

"I'd never have guessed. Since you're stuck with the truth, concoct a potentially truthful cover story. Most of the local population knows that the Storm Channel came to town to cover Gilda. Tell people that you're researching the *possibility* of doing a feature segment on the man who experienced a freak accident during the hurricane that did very little other damage when it visited Glory. That gives you a perfect entrée to ask questions about Richard Squires."

"You're devious."

"You don't know the half of it. But now that I think about my idea, it would actually make a dandy feature for the Storm Channel. It's chock-full of human interest, particularly if this guy was the saint that everyone claims he was."

"Hmm, you're right."

"When you sell the idea to Cathy, be sure to give your old friend Mimi the credit."

"What kind of questions do I ask?"

"Benign questions about Squires's life. Where did he grow up? Where did he go to school? Where was he married? Where did he get the recipes for his restaurant? What were his hobbies? What kind of home did he own? What kind of car did he drive? What did he like to—"

"I get the idea. Anything that pops into my mind about Richard's activities."

"Within limits. We don't need to know his shirt size." Mimi laughed. "The questions don't matter much because you don't care about the answers."

"Then why ask them?"

"Because the more routine questions you ask, the more likely people are to add the juicier details of Richard's life. I've never run across a saint who hasn't committed a sin or two."

"I owe you one, Mimi."

"By the time this is over, you'll owe me *several.* And I won't let you forget it."

Sean's excitement was soon diminished by the realization that although Mimi had provided an interviewing strategy, he had to locate the people to talk to. Two providential memories provided the solution.

Sean recalled Rafe saying that Richard sang in the Glory Community choir. He also remembered seeing a brochure about the choir in the Scottish Captain's front parlor. Sean assembled a list of singers, found the Glory white pages and reached for his cell phone. His first call was to the Glory Garage. Tucker Mackenzie confirmed that the Storm Channel broadcast van was roadworthy.

Sean assembled his interrogatory treasures at one of Emma Neilson's antique desks, where he transcribed the comments he'd captured with his digital audio recorder.

He'd been amazed by people's willingness to talk freely into a recording device. Mimi had been right about that as well as the ability of benign questions to draw out barbed observations about another human being. The pithy comments about Richard Squires fell into a natural order in Sean's notes:

"Richard wasn't as committed to the choir as he had once been. Last month he said, 'I have to devote more time to other things. There are changes in the works, and I'm not talking about a new way to cook grits.'"

"Richard said something strange to me during the break at choir rehearsal a few weeks ago. He said, 'Soon my life will change forever. Something I didn't think could ever happen has happened. It will surprise everyone.'"

"Most of us were surprised to see Richard coming to church with a new lady friend. Other than her, he didn't have much of a social life. Richard could be a hard person to warm up to. I don't think he had a lot of friends."

"He seemed to like Sheila, but not *that* much—if you know what I mean. He'd bring her to church once in a while, but I didn't think they were an item."

"Frankly, Richard could be downright moody. He often missed our mid-week choir practices."

"Richard was not always a good judge of character. Twenty-five years ago, he had a serious problem with a business partner, and ended up in court. And recently he'd been seeing the hostess at his restaurant. I think Sheila Parker is the kind of woman who can take serious advantage of a man like Richard. It's easy to see what she's after—M-O-N-E-Y."

Sean read through the comments twice, not sure what he had accomplished. At the very least, he was gathering fresh information.

He wished that Ann were here. She knew Richard Squires and might spot significant details that he'd overlooked. But mostly he just missed her.

The missing will get much worse—unless you find the motive and figure out how to change her mind.

TWELVE

Sean's cell phone rang at seven on Friday morning.

"How goes the pursuit of information?" Mimi Gallagher asked.

"Good, but not great."

"In other words, you've collected dribs and drabs of data, but nothing that lights up your life."

"Well…" Sean had to admit that Mimi's description nailed his modest achievements so far.

"Unsatisfactory!" She produced an irritated snort. "I expected more from you, Sean. I counted on your investigation to deliver the foundation of a usable feature segment for both our channels." To his surprise, her voice filled with honey. "The time has come to change your interrogation approach. What would you think of tapping a few telephones in Glory?"

Although Mimi punctuated her absurd suggestion with one of her signature laughs, Sean wasn't sure she was joking. She finally said, "Lighten up, Miller! We both know that you wouldn't recognize an electronic surveillance device if it jumped into your hand and chomped your finger. Given the woefully inadequate level of your education, your only practical course of action is to broaden your horizons and interview more folks who knew Richard Squires." She uttered a theatrical moan. "You *can* do that, can't you?"

"Definitely. But not until this afternoon. Glory will be shut down this morning. Most people are going to the funeral."

"Funeral? Whose funeral?"

"Richard Squires's—who else? It's scheduled for later this morning."

"Outstanding! The timing couldn't be better for our purposes."

"Really? I didn't plan to go."

"Don't be daft!" Mimi's voice was so loud that Sean had to pull his cell phone away from his ear. "Not only will you attend, you'll be the first mourner to arrive. There's no better circumstance than a funeral to observe the guest of honor's friends, family and acquaintances. And no better environment to overhear spicy tidbits of information about the deceased."

"I suppose…"

"You seem reluctant."

"Not at all," Sean fibbed. He had no intention of telling Mimi that he would have to explain his presence at Glory Community Church to Ann. She'd be annoyed to see him so soon after their "parting" the day before.

"Make sure you bring a camera with you," Mimi said. "Take photos of anyone you don't recognize. Strangers can be fruitful sources of information."

"Because…"

"Because they're people you haven't talked to yet, Sean."

"Taking pictures of people at a funeral is…intrusive."

"Not if you're discreet. Use the camera in your cell phone. And get the names of everyone you photograph."

"How do I do that?"

Her tone turned scolding. "For crying out loud, Sean, every guest at a funeral signs the condolence book. Shoot a picture of anyone you can't identify, and then peek at the page to see his or her name. Nothing could be easier."

"For you, but not for me," he murmured.

"I didn't hear what you said."

"Forget it, Mimi. I'll call you later, if I need more advice."

The funeral would begin at ten-thirty. Sean followed Mimi's instructions and began walking to the church at nine-thirty. He felt his composure drain away when he reached the front door. What would he say to Ann when they met? And how would he resist throwing his arms around her?

Look at the bright side: Ann can't yell at you—not inside a church during a funeral.

Sean chose a chair in the corner of the narthex, not far from the small wooden stand that held the condolence book. He hoped that his clothing—slacks, a sport coat and a knit shirt—would pass muster. It was the most formal outfit he took with him on field assignments and he hadn't had an opportunity to go shopping for something more funereal.

Sean quickly discovered that watching mourners sign the book and shooting the occasional candid photograph might actually be as simple as Mimi had predicted. But she'd left out an important detail. Most of the people he couldn't recognize weren't bona fide strangers. Townsfolk and members of Glory Community bubbled with self-assurance when they walked in and promptly greeted each other as old friends. He decided not to snap their photos.

The first non-Glorian arrived at 10:10 a.m., a man close to sixty, although Sean couldn't guess on which side of the divide he fell. The man had a lanky build, salt-and-pepper

hair and a weathered, leathery complexion. His gaze
shifted continuously, from guest to guest—he looked uncomfortable to be inside the narthex. He spoke to a woman
wearing a Can-I-Help-You badge; she pointed toward the
corridor that led to the church's offices. The man left
quickly, without signing the condolence book.

"What was that all about?" Sean muttered. He looked
at the photograph he'd taken and wondered who might
know the man's name.

At 10:15 a.m., two new strangers appeared: A husky
man in his early thirties and a slightly younger woman.
They seemed unsure about their surroundings and dili-
gently studied all the direction signs in view. Sean read
their condolence book signatures after they'd signed:
Jordan Squires, Austin, Texas and Mrs. Erin Squires
Bradshaw, San Antonio, Texas.

Sean winced at his lack of discernment. Jordan and
Erin were Richard's children. He should have recognized
them—they resembled the pictures he'd seen of their
father. All three Squires had narrow noses, prominent
cheekbones and deep-set eyes.

Sean looked around the narthex. If the locals knew
Richard's children, they'd chosen to leave them alone with
their grief before the funeral. Jordan and Erin were
standing together near the door to the sanctuary, peering
expectantly at people's faces.

Sean suddenly understood why. The two were waiting
for Miles Hayden. He'd been cloddish enough to arrange
a business meeting with them minutes before the funeral
service began. It had seemed odd when Hayden had talked
about it in Norfolk, but now that Richard's funeral was
about to begin, a meeting to discuss the future of Squires'
Place seemed disrespectful, even hardhearted.

On the other hand, the two Squires kids had agreed to the meeting.

A thought took shape in Sean's mind. *Ann is right; I am too judgmental. People grieve differently. If Jordan and Erin agreed to meet with Miles Hayden, perhaps they'd be willing to spend a few minutes talking with me about their father.*

Sean walked to the front door and looked outside. Hayden was nowhere to be seen. He moved quickly to Jordan and Erin. "I'm terribly sorry about your loss," he said. "I've come to appreciate your father's accomplishments in recent days. He was a fine man."

"Mr. Hayden?" Jordan asked.

"No, I'm Sean Miller." He pushed open the door of the empty sanctuary. Jordan and Erin followed him inside.

"Are you part of Mr. Hayden's development company?" Jordan said.

"No. I'm a field producer with the Storm Channel. I'm gathering information to help us decide whether we should produce a feature segment about your father's accident."

Sean found that the words flowed easily. They weren't quite false, if not exactly true although, if he had anything to do with future broadcasts, the Storm Channel would indeed develop a ten-minute feature about Richard Squires.

Jordan laughed. "Dad loved publicity of every kind. I'm sure he's looking down at us now, thrilled that Squires' Place might be featured on a TV show."

Sean said, "Folks in Glory say that Richard didn't exaggerate when he claimed to make the best grits in the South."

Erin joined in her brother's laughter. "Anyone who disagreed would have ended up in fistfight with Dad—or a grits-eating contest."

Sean tried for a neutral expression, then said, "I've heard that you plan to sell Squires' Place."

Jordan frowned and shook his head. "I don't know who told you that, but it's not true. We haven't begun to think about the future of the restaurant."

"He's obviously been talking to Miles Hayden," Erin said.

Sean decided to take a risk. "You're right, Mrs. Bradshaw. I visited Miles Hayden in Norfolk. What happens to Squires' Place deserves to be part of any feature about your father."

Sean held his breath. He sensed that Jordan was on the brink of chasing him away, but he finally shrugged. "None of this makes sense to me, but Hayden called the other day and said that he'd negotiated an arrangement with my dad to purchase the restaurant so he could construct some kind of professional building in Glory. Frankly, the idea of Dad selling Squires' Place astonished me so much that I barely heard the rest of what Hayden had to say."

"Your father hadn't told you of his ripening deal with Miles Hayden?"

"Not a hint, but that doesn't mean anything. Dad kept his own counsel about Squires' Place. We weren't in the loop." He smiled. "You see, we let him down. He tried to teach us the restaurant business, but I became a dentist and Erin a teacher."

Erin joined in. "However, Jordan and I proved to be our father's children. We both learned to cook spectacular grits."

Jordan looked at Sean. "When we saw you staring at us we thought you might be Hayden. Erin and I agreed to meet with him today, although I don't understand his rush. It will take months to settle Dad's estate. We don't even plan to talk to Dad's lawyer until next week."

Sean looked over his shoulder—still no Miles Hayden. He would take one more risk. "This may seem an odd question," he said, "but did your father ever talk about a relationship with a woman named Sheila Parker?"

"The hostess?"

Sean nodded. "She and Richard seemed to have been close—almost engaged, in fact. If we do a feature about your dad, she'll be part of it."

Erin shook her head. "Dad and I called each other regularly, perhaps once a week. A while ago he said that he'd hired a new hostess and liked her work, but he never mentioned anything about a budding romance."

"Ditto for me," Jordan said.

"Sheila claims that you put her in charge of Squires' Place."

"Not quite." Jordan frowned again. "We asked her to reopen the restaurant and watch over things for few days. She knows that it's only a temporary arrangement and that we intend to hire a permanent manager. She's in the running for the full-time job, but we aren't ready to offer it yet."

"Ah! Jordan and Erin! There you are." Sean took a step backward as Miles Hayden charged into the sanctuary. The developer managed the curious trick of smiling at Jordan and Erin but glaring at Sean more or less simultaneously.

Sean moved to the other side of the sanctuary, but he couldn't help overhearing Hayden say, "A thousand apologies. Traffic was much heavier than I'd anticipated." He made a show of looking at his watch. "We don't have time to talk before the service, but I know that you plan to stay in Glory for several days. I've checked into a local B and B myself, so I'm sure we'll find another chance to meet."

The guests had started to enter the sanctuary. Sean

walked to the back to find a bulletin that listed the order of worship and the hymns. He stopped abruptly when he saw Ann striding toward him.

"What are you doing here?" Her sharp tenor and confrontational demeanor fulfilled his earlier predictions.

"I'm attending Richard's funeral," he said evenly.

"Why? You've never met the man." She leaned forward as if spoiling for a fight. "We had a deal. You promised to stay away from me."

"You ordered me away. I never promised."

"I don't have time to split hairs with you. Overseeing this funeral is my last official duty at Glory Community Church. I won't settle for less than a flawless service and ceremony." She added, "I don't know why you're here, but it had better have nothing to do with finding a motive for murder. That game is over."

"Well, since you're curious, I'll be pleased to explain my presence. I'm on duty, too. For the Storm Channel."

"Have you looked outside? It's a beautiful day."

"True, but I'm working inside, to collect interesting information about Richard Squires. I may recommend that we produce a feature segment about him."

Her eyes narrowed. "Why?"

Once again, Mimi Gallagher came to his rescue. "Richard experienced a freak accident during a hurricane that did very little other damage when it visited Glory. A story like that is chock-full of human interest."

"You're serious about this?"

"Cross my heart," Sean said, sensing a small victory.

She sighed. "Don't bother the mourners."

"I promise I'll be good. I'm merely going to look and listen—and pray a little. Chiefly about you. You need the wisdom to rethink your impulsive decision to leave Glory."

"I'm at peace with all that has happened, and everything I plan to do."

She talked with conviction, but he didn't believe her. Once again the expression on her face spoke louder than her words. Anyone could make out that Ann loved her job at Glory Community Church and that she didn't want to be bullied out of Glory by Phil Meade.

From her vantage point in the front of the sanctuary, Ann could see Sean sitting on the right side and Phil Meade sitting on the left. Both men were staring intently at her.

Sean looked unhappy. Apparently he'd finally accepted that she would leave Glory. Ann knew she'd hurt and disappointed him. She hadn't meant to, but she knew that cutting off their relationship had been the right thing to do.

Phil, though, looked delighted. Ann could almost feel his glee. He'd obviously heard that she had resigned and was tickled that he had won. He probably couldn't wait to gloat about his triumph to Rafe and Daniel.

It wouldn't make any difference to her. She'd be in Asheville.

Daniel moved to the pulpit and turned on his microphone. "Jesus said, 'I am the resurrection and the life. He who believes in me will live, even though he dies.'"

Ann had helped Daniel plan a straightforward service with a reception immediately after in Fellowship Hall. She had heard Daniel officiate at dozens of funerals. Today, he followed the same simple three-element pattern he often adopted.

First, he offered thanks to God for the valuable life of the deceased and the impact he had on his family and friends. Second, he spoke frankly about the pain that death causes when it separates the deceased from his loved ones. Third, he emphasized that Jesus' resurrection demonstrates His victory over death—a victory that the Gospel teaches is ours in Christ.

Nina McEwen had selected, with Sheila Parker's input, three old and popular hymns, all of them among Ann's favorites: "Blessed Assurance," "Because He Lives" and "Amazing Grace."

Many guests asked to give eulogies, but Daniel limited the number to three. Joseph Lyman, Glory's mayor, praised Richard's lifelong love of Glory, his determination to outshine other Albemarle Sound towns, and how he had died serving the community. Jackson Wallace, the president of the Glory Chamber of Commerce, extolled Richard's commitment to the business community.

When the time came for Daniel to introduce the third speaker, he smiled toward the pews and said, "Our final message of remembrance this morning will be delivered by a speaker who asked me not to tell you his name. I'll merely say here's a gentleman who knew Richard Squires longer than almost anyone else in this sanctuary."

The man crossed in front of Ann as he walked to the podium. She'd never seen him before; she'd certainly have remembered his thick salt-and-pepper hair and his wrinkled face. He paused to adjust the height of his microphone and used the occasion to show his face to different parts of the sanctuary.

Ann listened to a trickle of murmured oohs from the pews. Some mourners looked bewildered, while others looked shocked. All seemed puzzled to see the third eulogizer standing at the podium.

"Good morning my friends," he began. "Most of you here today think of me as a new face at Glory Community

Church, but some of you know better. I'm anything but a new face. In fact, I used to live in Glory. I was baptized at Glory Community sixty-three years ago. I grew up in this church and was a member for more than thirty-five years. And then, one morning twenty-five years ago, I left Glory and swore that I'd never return."

The trickle of murmurs became a loud flood. Two people in the front row were glaring at the speaker.

"Ah," he said. "Several of you remember me. If so, you'll also recall the reason that I moved away. I left Glory because I hated Richard Squires."

A few guests booed and at least one shouted, "Get out!" The mourners might have become even noisier had Daniel not stepped in front of the pulpit and asked for quiet.

"I agree with you, my friends," the speaker went on. "*Hate* is a strong word. Unfortunately, it fit me perfectly. Back then I considered Richard Squires my worst enemy.

"My name, for those of you who don't recall it, is James Defoe. Richard and I grew up together. We were the best of friends in high school and best men at each other's weddings. And when Richard's children were born, I became their unofficial uncle. Richard and I were also partners in the restaurant business. If you look at the documents that founded Squires' Place, you'll see our names side by side. Our names show up side by side again—Defoe versus Squires—in the documents that launched the lawsuit I brought against Richard.

"What did we fight over? Money, of course. When we created Squires' Place, Richard provided the know-how, the creative ideas and his wonderful manner with customers. I provided the money, a large sum I'd inherited upon the death of my grandfather.

"We succeeded, thanks completely to Richard's efforts.

But I wasn't satisfied with reasonable profits. I insisted that we open a bigger restaurant in Elizabeth City. I believed that Glory was too small, that we'd never generate the kind of revenues we could in a bigger city.

"Alas, I never understood how important Squires' Place had become to Richard. To me, our restaurant was merely an investment. To Richard, it was a calling—the way he honored God."

Ann noticed Sean furiously jotting in his black notebook.

James Defoe continued, "We had a falling-out and decided to end our partnership. In 1982, Richard bought out my share of our partnership and I left Glory to open my own restaurant in Elizabeth City. But I grew unhappy with what Richard had paid me. I felt shortchanged, convinced that he had cheated me. The court decided that Richard had paid enough, but that only made me hate him more."

Sean caught Ann's eye. She knew what he was thinking. Here was a man with real motive for murder. Revenge. A feud that had lasted more than twenty-five years? She could practically hear Sean saying, *You told me that Richard didn't have enemies.* Well, she hadn't known about James.

Defoe talked on. "When I left Glory, I also left Christianity. I foolishly spent twenty-five years hating Richard Squires, doing much more damage to myself than to him. Naturally my own restaurant failed. I was so full of hatred I could barely smile at my customers.

"My testimony about Richard is simple. Despite everything I did, he never hated me. He often tried to reach me— by phone, by mail, through mutual acquaintances—all with the intent of restoring our relationship. I rebuffed him again and again.

"Until two years ago. That's when I became a Christian all over again—a real Christian. I'm delighted to report that this past summer, Richard and I restored our lost friendship. We even talked about me moving back to Glory and working with him at Squires' Place, just like the old days.

"To celebrate, I made us each an Eat Grits cap in our favorite colors. Mine is white with a red brim, his is red with a white brim. Richard told me that he wore it often in Glory." Defoe tugged a red-and-white baseball cap out of his jacket pocket and pulled it down on his head.

Ann shuddered. Defoe's cap was a version of the cap Richard had worn when he repaired the generator.

Defoe continued, "I suppose that every story told in church needs a moral. My moral is simple—be like Richard Squires, not like me. He knew what was important in life. He was loving, forgiving and loyal—to people who didn't deserve it." He brushed away a tear. "That sounds like God's grace, doesn't it? Richard, we'll miss you."

No one booed when Defoe finished talking. It was silent in the church except for a torrent of sniffs. Ann moved quickly along the side aisle; the service was almost over and she needed to make certain that the Fellowship Room was ready.

When the crowd of mourners arrived, so did Sean.

"We have to talk," he said. "What James Defoe said changes everything. I've been looking for a murder motive in the wrong place."

"It still makes no difference," Ann replied.

"Sure it does. Motive is the first step toward understanding what happened on Monday night. I care about this, Ann. And I'm sure they will also."

He cocked his head toward Jordan and Erin, who comprised a short receiving line near the front door. They were locked in a group hug with James Defoe. Several other guests were waiting to pay their respects.

"Hey! I have to talk to her," Sean said, spotting Sheila at the refreshment table.

"If she kicks you, I'm going to applaud."

"You'd like that, wouldn't you?"

Sean thought he saw a small smile on Ann's face as she walked with him toward Sheila. Sheila—busy heaping hors d'oeuvres on a paper plate—didn't see Sean approach.

He dove in. "Several people I've talked to know about your relationship with Richard, but no one knew how far along it had progressed."

Sheila used a canapé to wave away Sean's remark. "I told you—we decided to keep our engagement a secret."

"That's the thing. Even if you hadn't talked about it, people would have noticed the signs. But no one did."

"You have a whale of a lot of nerve to gossip about me in Glory." She tossed a handful of canapé dust at Sean. "Stay away from me. We have nothing else to talk about."

"Oh, yes we do. I want to look at Richard's paperwork, especially the documents pertaining to any potential sale of Squires' Place."

"That'll never happen."

"Never say never. I intend to ask Richard's children for permission to browse through his papers at the restaurant— the documents you've organized so neatly in the file room."

She glared at Sean, an ugly glower that seemed close to rage.

"What you do or don't do is no concern of mine." She stormed off with her plateful of food.

"Wow!" Ann said, "You seem to have lost a friend."

"I'll say." He laughed. "And here I thought you were the only woman I could make mad."

Ann noticed that Sheila stopped halfway across the room to look back at Sean.

If looks could kill...

THIRTEEN

"Are you sure about this, Daniel?" Ann smiled at him, wondering what had prompted his last-minute invitation to dinner.

"Absolutely positively sure," he said. "We'll expect you at seven."

"And Lori is okay with this?" she asked, wary of interrupting a still-honeymooning couple.

He laughed. "'We' is Lori and me."

Ann couldn't hear any waffling or insincerity in his voice, but his unexpected request bewildered her. Daniel wasn't a last-minute kind of person. Retired army colonels liked to plan things in advance. But this invitation had been entirely spontaneous. They'd been chatting after Richard's funeral, when out of the blue a strange look crossed Daniel's face. "Have dinner with us tonight," he'd said.

In the end, Ann accepted, as graciously as her fears of being a gloomy table companion would allow. "I'd be delighted to come to dinner, Daniel, even though I won't be the best of company this evening. I set aside this afternoon to pack up my office. I'm already feeling a tad melancholy."

"I understand completely. Lori and I will do our best to cheer you up. We've both done lots of spur-of-the-moment moving around ourselves. Packing in a hurry can be a real pain."

What an odd thing for Daniel to say, Ann thought, as she struggled to keep the smile on her face. She reminded herself that Daniel had lots on his mind, too. He clearly wanted to be supportive, even if he expressed himself awkwardly.

Friday afternoon passed in a flurry of corrugated cardboard boxes, plastic packing tape and trips to her car to load her belongings. Ann called the manse a few minutes before seven and spoke to Daniel. "Can I bring anything this evening? Extra soft drinks or dessert?"

"Nope. We have everything we need. Simply bring yourself."

"Myself is on the way."

Ann endured yet another twinge of remorse when she put down the phone. Cleaning out her office—wrapping her collection of framed photographs—had triggered a steady succession of bittersweet feelings. She'd miss lots of things in Glory, but she'd Daniel and Glory Community Church most of all.

She snatched up her car keys, determined to be resolute that evening. No gnashing of teeth. No crying. She'd made a sensible decision; there was no turning back. She regretted leaving her job, but in time all good things came to an end. That was how the world worked. She switched off the lights in her office for the last time as church administrator.

Ann tapped hesitantly on the front door to the manse. *Cheer up, or you'll ruin Daniel and Lori's Friday evening.* Daniel opened the door and Lori scooted gracefully around him to give Ann a brawny, welcoming hug.

"Welcome to Chez Hartman," she said. "You're our first dinner guest as a married couple."

"I'm honored," Ann said, breathless from the hug. Lori was strong as well as nimble. When they first met, Ann had thought Lori too elegant—and too pretty—to be a police officer, but then Lori talked about her twelve years as a special agent in the U.S. Army's Criminal Investigation Division. This decidedly unusual pastor's wife would soon join the Glory Police Department as a detective.

Ann detected a familiar odor in the foyer. She sniffed. "I know that delicious smell, but I can't put a name to it."

"That's our dinner," Daniel said. "Cheesy shrimp and grits, à la Squires' Place."

"But that was one of Richard's most secret recipes."

"It's not secret anymore," Lori said. "Calvin Constable, Emma Neilson's breakfast chef, 'reverse engineered' the ingredients. He's a genius at identifying different spices."

"Cheesy shrimp and grits is one of my favorites."

"I know," Daniel said. "That's why I asked Lori to prepare it. I wanted your last home-cooked meal in Glory to be memorable. You won't have much opportunity to eat Glory-style grits in the future."

Ann stared at the foyer's bare wood floor. Daniel was right, but couldn't he have found a more tactful way to voice what he'd said?

"How about a glass of lemonade?" Lori asked.

"I'd love some," Ann answered.

"You two head for the dining room. I'll join you in a minute."

Daniel gave Lori a military salute. "Yes, ma'am." Then he offered Ann his arm and escorted her into the dining room.

Ann was familiar with the furniture in the manse, but

there was something different about the dining room this evening. The table setting wasn't elaborate, but the splash of late-summer flowers in the center and the charmingly folded napkins tucked into tall lemonade glasses sang of a woman's touch.

"Lori sets a wonderful table," Ann said. "I'm impressed."

"Me, too!" Daniel said with a smile. "She's adjusting to me faster than I thought possible. Everything's new to Lori. Becoming a pastor's wife, managing a household, transforming my bachelor manse into a convivial home. She's taken every challenge of our marriage in stride."

Ann nodded. If Lori could transition from her thoroughly independent life to domestic tranquility, perhaps Ann could do the same thing someday, when the right man came along. She thought of Sean, but quickly dismissed him from her mind. Their lives had gone in different directions and that was that.

Daniel poured a glass of lemonade for Ann. A moment later, Lori arrived with a vast bowl of steaming cheesy shrimp and grits. She set it on an insulated pad made of cork.

"I'll give thanks for our food," Daniel said. "Heavenly Father, we thank You for the food and for the loving hands that prepared it. We also thank You for this time of fellowship with Ann. We'll miss her, but we know that she thought carefully about her life and has made the right decision for her future. In Jesus' name we pray. Amen."

Ann said a soft "amen." At last, Daniel had understood that she'd looked at every possible alternative and reached the only conclusion that made sense. Leaving Glory was the right decision for her future.

Lori handed Ann a large spoon. "Dig in—and don't be

shy. I accidentally made enough cheesy shrimp and grits to feed our choir. Calvin didn't provide scaling directions along with his recipe."

Ann served herself and inched the bowl toward Daniel.

"I won't kid you, Ann," he said, as he filled his plate. "I tossed and turned most of last night. For the first three hours, I couldn't bear to contemplate the thought of you leaving Glory Community Church. But then I thought some more." He stroked his chin thoughtfully. "I began to realize that you made the right decision to sacrifice your career. If you keep working at Glory Community Church, your presence could easily start World War III in the pews."

Ann nodded in agreement. "The last thing I want to do is be responsible for a fight among members of the congregation."

"It's a terrible shame really, but all we can do is face reality and recognize the foibles of human nature." Daniel shook his head glumly. "Like it or not, you've become a disruptive force inside the church. And so, the only solution is for you to leave. I wish it were otherwise, but that's the way people are—they take sides. We live in a fallen Creation and must expect the church's flock to occasionally exhibit foolish and outrageous behavior. All you can do is admit defeat."

Ann poked at a shrimp with her fork. Daniel's words weren't what she expected to hear. He clearly understood the problem and the high price she was about to pay. But should an experienced pastor give up so easily? She expected him to have a few thoughts about a solution—not that he could change her mind.

Wasn't it the pastor's job to teach the elders the dangers of faultfinding and to counsel the congregation not to take sides? Why not deliver a sermon or two on what Jesus thought about hypocrites who ignored their own short-comings and attacked others? Daniel could have built an exciting homily around a verse she'd recently memorized for a Bible study: Jesus asked, "Why do you look at the speck of sawdust in your brother's eye and pay no attention to the plank in your own eye?"

Lori broke into Ann's musings. "Have you finalized your plans for the future?"

Ann gave an uncertain shrug. "Not really. In the short term, Mom and I will stay at my brother's home in Asheville. We need time to consider the different choices we have."

"That's right, I'd forgotten," Daniel said. "You moved back to Glory last year to take care of your mother." He brought his hands apart in a puzzled gesture. "Whatever you decide, I'm certain that your mother will adapt quickly to her new surroundings."

Ann nodded quickly. "Oh yes, Mother is very flexible." But even as she spoke the words, she wished that Daniel had not reminded her about her mother's increasing need for live-in support. Mom loved Glory—and her house—and would be reluctant to leave permanently. Well, that was another dilemma Ann would have to resolve in the days ahead.

Again it was Lori who interrupted Ann's thoughts. "Have you thought about a new job yet?"

"No. I'm leaning toward returning to school and earning an MBA, but if I find a new full-time job, it won't be a position that puts me in the public spotlight. I have limitations because of my past."

"Limitations," Daniel echoed. "Yes, I understand the way you feel. The past can definitely be a burden on the present. And you'd be wise to avoid a job that involves significant responsibility. You never know when you might run into another Phil Meade."

Ann felt a new wrench of annoyance at Daniel. He didn't have to be so willing to agree with her. Worse yet, it sounded as if he thought Phil Meade was right. Baloney! Even though she had decided not to fight with him for the good of the church, Phil was unreservedly mistaken about her past and her present.

"I've been pondering, Ann," Daniel said. "Even though Phil isn't a member of Glory Community, I might ask him to participate on the search committee that looks for your replacement. Do you have an opinion?"

"Don't you dare!" Ann tried to say, but the words caught in her throat and was something between a growl and a roar.

"I'm sorry the idea upsets you," Daniel said, "but think it through. There's a good reason to involve Phil. The three elders whom he swayed might be more favorably disposed to a candidate if they knew that Phil had been part the selection process."

Ann felt foolish for losing her cool. Daniel was right; she hadn't thought through any of the practical aspects of her resignation, including the obvious question of who would replace her.

"Daniel, I didn't mean to leave you in the lurch. Would you like me to help you find a church administrator to succeed me?"

Daniel smiled. "Thank you, Ann, but there's no need to revise your plans this late in the day. I'll put a help-wanted ad in the *Glory Gazette* on Monday. That should do the trick. After all, church administration isn't rocket science."

A fresh blast of indignation made Ann sit up in her seat. "How dare you say something that insensitive to me?

In fact, you've been spouting tactless comments all evening, Daniel. What's gotten in to you?"

Daniel shrugged. "I merely said the words you wanted me to say—the words *you* put in my mouth with your one-sided decision to leave Glory Community Church."

"But—"

Daniel went on. "You never asked for my opinion. You just marched into my office and announced that you had decided to leave."

"But we both agreed that my staying might trigger a battle within the elder board."

"No 'might' about it. There would have been a fight. But that's one of the reasons the congregation pays me the big bucks to be Pastor of Word and Sacrament." He began to grin. "It's my job to deal with people who act like people. I'd have let the upset elders fret and fume for a while, but not allowed the disagreement to spill over into the congregation. I'm convinced that there'll come a point in God's good time when Phil Meade and company will recognize that you had nothing to do with Richard Squires's death."

Ann shifted uncomfortably in her seat.

"For the record, it grieves me to see you give in to Phil Meade," Daniel continued. "He's behaved like a bully toward you, as Sean Miller aptly demonstrated at yesterday's meeting." Daniel's expression brightened. "Did you notice how Sean lit up when he defended you? You must have seen the fire in his eyes—a glow fueled by his feelings for you."

Ann felt herself blushing. The criticism that Daniel had leveled against her could have also been voiced by Sean. She'd made her decision to leave Glory without asking his wishes. But why should Sean have a say in the matter? There was no way around the messy truth that he was based in Long Island, while she lived in North Carolina.

Still, Ann had to admit that Sean had defended her, had taken on the role of her champion. Moreover, she'd become fond of his curious blend of confidence and insecurity, of boldness and shyness. He could make her laugh—and when he'd kissed her, she'd returned his kiss. Happily.

Ann looked at her empty plate. "That was delicious. Can I help with the dishes?"

Lori laughed. "Absolutely not. Daniel is in training for our busboy job. You stay put. I hope you saved room for dessert."

"Well—"

"Did someone mention dessert? Here it is!"

Ann's heart began to thump when she recognized Sean Miller's voice. She swiveled in her chair and saw Sean holding a half-gallon tub of Rocky Road ice cream.

It seems I'm the victim of a conspiracy.

Sean realized that he'd started grinning the moment he saw the astonished look on Ann's face. But amusement was not the emotion he wanted to convey to her right now.

"I brought your favorite," he said. "It won't solve any of your underlying problems, but it will make you feel better, maybe even make you think that you're in control of your life."

Ann recoiled as if she'd been slapped. "If you're going to deliver another pompous lecture," she said, "wait until we're alone."

"An excellent point," Lori said to Daniel. "Two's company, four is…"

"Way too many." Daniel cleared away the dirty dishes.

Lori carried the bowl of cheesy shrimp and grits to the kitchen. She poked her head around the kitchen door and winked. "Let the pompous lecture begin."

Ann held up her hands. "You don't have to tell me that neither you nor Daniel wants me to leave Glory. I've figured that out for myself."

Sean shook his head. "I stood in the kitchen while you and Daniel were talking. Everything you said to him proves that *you* don't want to leave Glory. You just need someone to talk you out of quitting your job. That's my responsibility tonight. I'm here to make you an offer you can't refuse."

Ann peered at him quizzically. "And that would be?"

Sean reached into a pocket and retrieved a rolled-up piece of parchment paper—tied with a loop of black ribbon—that he'd carefully fashioned to resemble a scroll. He presented it to Ann. She undid the ribbon, flattened the scroll on the dining room table and began to laugh when she read:

Dear Ann,
I'll be handling your problems from now on. I won't need your help—so have a great life in Glory. By the way, I love you…and so does Sean Miller!
Love,
God

"Okay," she said, poking the scroll with a finger. "You've got me convinced that I need to *'let go, let God.'* I made my decision to leave Glory on my own. It was a mistake and I've learned my lesson. But I'm confused. What's the offer I can't refuse?"

"Me. The man who brings you Rocky Road." Sean reached across the table and placed his hand over hers. "I'm also the man who's fallen in love with you."

Ann withdrew her hand and placed it in her lap, out of

his reach. "Sean, you just talked me into staying in Glory, but you live and work on Long Island. I have my mother to take care of and you have your student loans to pay back. Those are genuine issues we can't ignore. What are we going to do about them?"

Sean stood and moved close to Ann. She didn't resist as he urged her to her feet and put his arms around her. She leaned her head against his shoulder and he could feel her start to tremble.

"*We're* not going to do anything about them," he said, as he hugged her tightly. "Heavenly Father," he said, "thank You for bringing Ann into my life. I love her very much and I hope that she loves me in return. That, of course, is in Your hands. We give our future to You—in full confidence that the God who created the Universe can solve the relatively minor problem of where we'll live and work. In Jesus' name we pray. Amen."

"Amen and amen." Ann began to chuckle. "Now I feel like a complete idiot."

"For?"

"For not trusting God, for refusing to admit to myself that I do love you and for acting the way I did about Carlo Vaughn."

"Now there's a problem we can solve by ourselves. If we ever have a home with cable TV, I intend to block the Storm Channel."

She giggled. He tilted her head so that he could see her face.

"Are you happy?" Sean asked.

"Of course. I'm also excited. I can't wait to find out how God will sort out our lives for us."

"Did I say that I love you, dear?" He clapped his hand over his mouth. "Oops. I shouldn't have said that."

"Said what—said that you love me?"

"No. You don't like being called 'dear.'"

"I will make an exception for you, because I love you, too, Sean."

Sean lowered his face toward Ann's and kissed her. She returned his kiss, putting her arms around him. He drew her closer, knowing that his life was changing. For the better. He had found his soul mate at last. *Thank you, Gilda.*

Sean sensed motion behind him. "Don't let me interrupt you," Daniel said. "I've just come back for my ice cream."

Ann began to laugh. All Sean could do was join in.

FOURTEEN

Ann lifted an overflowing cardboard carton out of her sedan's backseat and struggled toward Glory Community Church's side door. Halfway there, she remembered that the key was in her handbag, which hung from her right shoulder. She balanced the awkward load on her left hip and delved for her key with her right hand.

All at once, the carton began to slip. She tried to grab hold of it but felt the box slide away from her body, out from under her arm.

Instead of the crash she expected to hear, Sean said, "I thought you might need a hand."

She twirled around. "Are you following me?" she said with a smile.

"Actually, I've started to understand how you think." He propped the carton on his shoulder and broke into a self-satisfied grin. "I reckoned that you'd want to restore your office first thing this morning."

As he leaned toward her, she slipped away. "No kissing in the church parking lot."

"Sheesh! Glory Community has too many rules."

"That's *my* rule. As you wisely concluded, my top priority this morning is to put all my stuff back in my office." She touched the tip of his nose. "Talk to me about kissing when we're finished."

"In that case, unlock the door. This box is getting heavy."

The seventh and last carton they moved into Ann's office contained a potpourri of her belongings, from a coffeemaker to an assortment of decorative objects.

"Wow!" Sean said, "I haven't seen one of those in decades. My great-grandmother had some hanging in her house. I even forget what they're called."

"An embroidered sampler."

"I didn't know that people made them anymore."

"My mother still makes them—"

"Oops."

"—as gifts for friends and family. She gave me this one when I finished college. She embroidered her favorite Bible verse, 'Whatever you do, work at it with all your heart, as working for the Lord, not for men.'"

"That's close to what James Defoe said yesterday," Sean said. "Richard thought of Squires' Place as his calling—the way he honored God."

"Everyone should feel that way about his or her job."

Ann looked at Sean, expecting a reply. But his gaze had fixed on the sampler and he seemed lost in thought.

"I began thinking about this yesterday," he finally said. "A man like Richard would never sell his means to honor God. No matter what."

Ann remembered what Sean had told her the day before, although she'd all but ignored his comment at the time. "What James Defoe said changes everything. I've been looking for a murder motive in the wrong place," Sean had said.

Everything seemed to fall into place in her mind. In a single exuberant beat of her heart, she understood what Sean had tried to tell her.

"The two of them—Hayden and Sheila—are working together. They killed Richard Squires," Ann said, her eyes wide.

"Without doubt. We should have realized they were capable of committing murder the first time we spoke to them."

"I didn't like him when we talked. Or her."

"Me neither. Doing business during a funeral should have been our initial clue about Hayden."

"It's so transparent," Ann said. "You were right, Sean. Someone did have a reason to kill Richard."

"Avarice is one of the oldest motives for murder in the book."

"The signs were there all the time, but we just didn't see them."

"I don't feel so foolish that we ignored the obvious," Sean said with a chuckle. "So did Rafe."

"Speaking of Rafe, shouldn't we tell him what we've figured out?"

"At once, if not sooner." He read his watch. "It's nine-twenty. At this time of morning, unless an unexpected crime wave hit Glory, he'll be at police headquarters or the Scottish Captain."

"Shall we walk or drive?"

"Drive of course. I'm bushed from all the heavy lifting you required me to perform this morning."

"Poor baby." Ann gave Sean a peck on his cheek.

"Aha!" he said. "Kissing is allowed in the church administrator's office."

"You call that a kiss?"

"Now that you mention it…" He stretched to grasp her hand.

Ann sprang out his reach. "Rafe awaits."

Sean followed her out of the church. "So do I."

They were both laughing when they got into Ann's car. Consequently, neither Ann nor Sean noticed Miles Hayden scrunched down in the backseat until he sat up and pointed a small black pistol at the back of Sean's head.

"Start the engine," Miles said to Ann. "Drive slowly and carefully to the alley behind Squires' Place." He added, "Be sure to fasten your seat belts. After all, we don't want to do anything that might attract the police."

Ann felt her heart thumping. She glanced at Sean. He looked as fearful as she felt. And why not? As Rafe Neilson had so sagely observed, the person who killed Richard Squires wouldn't hesitate to kill again.

"Don't keep me waiting, Ann," Miles said. "Patience is not one of my virtues."

She turned the key, praying that this one time the engine would fail to start. Unfortunately, it growled to life.

She shifted into Drive and headed for Oliver Street. The journey to Squires' Place seemed to take no time at all. She pulled into the alley and parked near the middle.

"I'll get out of the car first," Miles said. "Then you two walk to the door. Resist the temptation to be a hero. Shooting you will be an inconvenience, but if it becomes necessary, I will do it."

Ann watched Miles move to the front of the car, where he had a good view of both her and Sean. Nothing that Ann could see tempted her toward heroism. Not yet, anyway.

Ann walked toward the steel door; she knew that Sean was close behind. His presence comforted her even though they were equally helpless against Miles's gun.

"Ring the bell," Miles said, "then move away from the door."

Sean pressed the button and stepped backward. The heavy door swung open without delay.

"Clasp your hands behind your back and walk inside slowly. Don't touch the door. If either of you even brush against it, I'll start shooting."

Ann waited inside the shadowy corridor, a few feet away from Sean. She flinched at the bang as Miles slammed the steel door shut.

Lord, I'm new at turning my problems over to You, but Sean and I are trapped in this building with a madman who's threatening us with a gun. We definitely need Your help.

Ann's eyes adjusted to the dim light. Sheila must have opened the door, but she was nowhere to be seen. Miles ordered them down the corridor and into Squires' Place dining room. Only a few overhead lights were on, throwing the perimeter of the large room in darkness. He pointed to an open area in the center of the floor, with two wooden chairs, roughly five feet apart. Ann took the chair on the right, Sean the chair on the left. Miles sat in a third chair about ten feet distant—far enough away to make "heroics" impossible, and close enough to insure an easy shot. He didn't even bother to issue another warning.

"Now there's a sight worth seeing," Sheila said, stepping out of the darkness. "They're not acting haughty today, are they? The snotty church lady and the nasty little gossip. It's a treat to watch them squirm."

Ann heard Sean shift in his chair. She could almost feel the anger coming off his body.

Dear God, don't let him do something foolish.

"What should we call you?" Sean asked. "I'm guessing your name isn't really Sheila."

"No. My name is Gail. Gail Hayden, to be specific. Does that surprise you?"

"Not really. It makes sense that you two are married."
Sean paused a moment. "Besides, Miles doesn't seem
bright enough to have designed this complex scheme by
himself. I think that you're the brains of this outfit."

Gail cackled gleefully. Miles fired a bullet into the floor
a few inches from Sean's right foot.

"Safety tip," Miles said. "Never offend a man who's
pointing a gun at you."

The roar of the gunshot made Ann's ears ring. She
muttered a silent prayer that someone nearby had heard the
shot and would report it to the police.

Miles waved away the small puff of gun smoke near his
chair. "Don't get your hopes up. This room is virtually
soundproof. The combination of the wood walls, the thick
stone facing, and the lack of windows means that what
happens in Squires' Place stays in Squires' Place. Get it?"
He laughed.

Sean said, "That's a thirty-two automatic, isn't it?"

"I'm impressed—the man knows his pistols," Miles
said to Gail. He waved the weapon at Ann and Sean. "By
today's standards, this isn't a big gun. But there are seven
more cartridges inside, each one more than powerful
enough to kill you. So pay close attention to everything we
say."

Ann knew what she had to do. Miles was too busy
showing off to pay attention to what her nervous fingers
were doing. Her chief threat came from Gail. But if the
woman thought that Ann was afraid of her, she might
ignore Ann and focus on Sean. It wasn't a sure thing, but
it was the only strategy Ann could implement while Miles
had his gun trained on them.

Ann averted her eyes. *Look frightened and she'll think
you are frightened. Lord, please let it work.*

"Why did you bring us here?" Ann emphasized the tremor in her voice. "Is that gun really necessary?"

"My my!" Sheila said, "Miss Trask isn't cocky anymore. She's downright petrified."

Ann tried to make her breathing echo her terrified expression. She knew that her behavior would upset Sean, but she prayed that he would catch on, or at least not do anything to throw attention on her hands.

"I don't hear any more clever insults from you this morning," Gail said. "Well, I wonder how clever you'll be when you find yourself part of Glory's latest urban renewal project."

"What are you talking about?" Ann asked.

Sean answered her question. "They're going to destroy Squires' Place."

"One convenient accident," Miles said, "will eliminate all our problems simultaneously—including you."

"Richard Squires refused to sell you his property, didn't he?" Sean asked.

"He seemed interested a year ago," Miles said, "but then he started dragging his heels after I'd invested a fortune in planning, site surveys and preliminary architectural work."

"But then one of you came up with the idea to send Gail to Glory, to spy on Richard," Sean said.

"That was my idea," Gail said. She winked at Sean. "You got it right *darlin'*, I am the brains of this outfit."

Sean braced himself for another shot at the floor, but Miles merely laughed.

"What can I say? My wife is an amazing lady. She cozied up to Richard Squires and wormed her way into his life. You have to admit, she pulled off a stunning accomplishment, becoming the hostess of this red-and-white eyesore."

"Absolutely dazzling," Sean agreed. "And what she learned on the job was that Richard Squires never intended to sell his restaurant."

Miles shrugged. "How was I supposed to know that he was some sort of religious nut? My situation became even more precarious when Richard decided to make friends again with James Defoe. Richard planned to expand Squires' Place with Defoe's help."

"So you decided to kill Richard," Sean said.

"I didn't have a choice," Miles said. "Besides spending lots of money, I'd already brought serious investors on board and made promises I had to keep." He made a sweeping motion with his right arm that took in the whole dining room. "When you start a major development project like this, you have to follow through."

"And now that Richard is dead, your next step will be to destroy this building. Right?"

"No more questions!" Gail shouted. She scowled at Miles. "These two don't need to know all our secrets."

"Don't be a wet blanket," he replied. "In another hour or two it won't make any difference what they know. And their curiosity is keeping me from getting bored. We still have lots of time to kill." Hayden laughed. "Get it. Time to kill?"

"You get more simpleminded each day," she said.

"You need to work on your sense of humor." Miles gestured at Sean with his pistol. "To answer your question, once we turn Squires' Place into a heap of rubble, Jordan and Erin will rush to sell me the property."

"I see your point," Sean said. "Destroying Squires' Place makes their decision easy. They won't worry as much about their father's wishes, or have to consider his promises to James Defoe. But what I can't work out is how you plan to demolish such a substantial building."

Miles smiled. "Substantial buildings burn down every day. There's so much wood, paper and cooking oil inside this restaurant that it will burn like the proverbial torch. All that heat will weaken the structure and the walls will come tumbling down." He added, "Jordan and Erin will collect a hefty payoff from the insurance company and I'll pick up Squires' Place at a fire-sale price. Literally! Everybody wins."

"Except for you two." Gail cackled once more. "At eleven-thirty this morning, time runs out for Ann Trask and Sean Miller."

"I'll bite," Sean said. "Why such a specific time?"

"Say *'pretty please'* and I may tell you."

"Two reasons," Ann said. "First, they want to start the fire before the staff arrives to start cooking. Squires' Place is supposed to reopen for dinner this evening.

"Second, they want to make the fire look like an accident. I'd guess they'll try to simulate a short in the electrical wiring. In a few minutes they'll switch on the fryers, coffee urns, hot plates and other appliances."

"And then at eleven-thirty, when everything is hot, BOOM!" Miles said, slamming his hands together.

Gail glared at Ann. "All of a sudden you seem to know a whole lot about restaurants."

"Glory Community Church has a commercial kitchen that we use to prepare meals for weddings and other events."

Gail uttered an exceptionally malevolent cackle. "By noon today your kitchen administering days will be over—and your ability to muddy the waters in someone else's pond."

Ann wrapped her arms around herself even more tightly. She clenched her right hand over her chest and forced herself to start trembling.

Gail went on, "I hope you realize that all of this is your own fault. You brought it on yourself when you started talking to people in Glory, when you kept asking questions. You even spoke to Richard's children at his funeral and stirred the pot some more."

"That was me," Sean said, "not Ann. Let her go."

"I don't think so," Gail said, with a singsongy intonation. She peered at Sean. "Your little friend is terrified, but you don't seem especially worried. Why is that?"

"You've made so many mistakes so far, I'm confident you'll bungle whatever you've planned for today."

"Mistakes?" Miles leaned forward in his chair, clearly annoyed. "Show me a single mistake we made."

"Well, for one, you didn't move Richard's car. You left it in the rear of the church's parking lot. It's obvious that he wasn't walking toward it when he was supposedly killed by the falling steeple."

Ann spotted Gail glowering at Miles and deduced what must have happened. "Miles forgot to take Richard's car keys out of his pocket before burying him under the wreckage," Ann said. "And then you saw Sean walking from the van to the church. You didn't want to risk poking around in the rubble, so you left Richard's car where he'd parked it."

"We won't make that mistake a second time." Gail held Ann's handbag aloft. "I made a point of retrieving your car keys."

"Even so," Ann said, "the fire department will find us."

"You mean that they'll find what's left of you in the ashes after the ruins cool down," Gail said. "But what if they do find you? Half the people in Glory know that you and your boyfriend are obsessed with proving that you're not responsible for Richard's death. That's why you snuck into Squires' Place to look through Richard's paperwork.

You foolishly locked yourself in the file room and couldn't get out when the accidental electrical fire started." She cackled yet again. "What a tragedy. Both of you—toast!"

"Let me share another mistake you made, Miles," Sean said. "After you clobbered Richard, you positioned him flat on his back, then covered him with rubble. He wouldn't have fallen that way."

"I told you not to place him faceup on the pavement," Miles said to Gail, "but you insisted."

"Of course I insisted. We had no way of knowing what the correct orientation for his body might be, so the simplest position was best. Getting fancy can get you caught."

"You promised that you'd never quote another line from that stupid textbook on detecting you read at the Glory Library."

Ann had to hide her laughter behind a sudden coughing fit.

Sean knew Ann was up to something, but he couldn't figure out what. He'd stolen several glances at her face; one moment she seemed terrified, the next completely at ease.

Figure it out later, he told himself. *Right now, you have to focus your entire being on getting that gun away from Miles Hayden.*

Miles and his wife weren't the sharpest knives in the drawer, but they'd been able to murder Richard at the height of a hurricane—and convince most of Glory that he'd died an accidental death. Their plan to burn down Squires' Place with Ann and him locked in the file room could easily succeed. Sean knew that at most he'd get one opportunity to wrench the gun out of Miles's hand; he'd have to be ready to act decisively when that time came.

Sean studied Miles's face. Discussing his mistakes

seemed to have dampened his enthusiasm for more time-killing questions. He frowned when Ann raised her hand. "What do you want?" he said.

"Can I use the bathroom before you lock us in the file room?"

Gail immediately replied. "Sure you can, honey. I'd hate for you to die thinking of us as unkind."

"Don't try anything," Miles said. "My gun is aimed at your boyfriend."

"What can she try? It's an ordinary ladies' room. Everything's bolted to the wall, and there's one door and no windows."

Sean managed to catch a glimpse of Ann's face as she stood up. Her bright eyes told the tale. She wanted to use the ladies' room for other than the usual reasons.

What did she plan to do? And how would Miles and Sheila react?

He held his breath as Ann walked toward the Gritty Gal's Room. Miles looked her way once or twice, but didn't appear concerned by her demeanor.

Sean began to count slowly to himself. Ann emerged from the ladies' room when he reached 164. The look on her face had become almost blissful. How could Miles or Gail not notice the change?

A doorbell rang.

"That's the back door," Gail said.

The bell rang again.

"The cook staff's not supposed to arrive until one." Miles stared angrily at his wife. "I can't trust you to do anything right."

"That's not the cook staff—" Her explanation was interrupted by a heavy thumping on the steel door that reverberated throughout the dining room.

"Get back there," Miles said. "Shout through the door. Tell whatever nitwit's out there to go away."

As Gail stood up, Ann said, "Sorry, but that won't work. It's the police. If you don't let them in, they'll break the door down."

The thumping became louder.

"Don't lie to me!" Miles hurdled out of his chair. "You had no way to contact anyone."

Ann held up the blue almond-shaped object hanging from the lanyard around her neck.

"That's not a telephone."

"Correct. It's a miniature tactical police radio."

Sean could hear the sound of tearing metal along with the thumping.

"The door's about to give way," Ann said.

Gail slapped the back of her husband's head, knocking his toupee to the floor. "You idiot! You fool! You're supposed to know about radios! You're a man!"

Sean watched the veins on Miles's temple throb as his face went red with fury. Miles moved toward Ann and raised his pistol.

Dear God! Don't let him shoot Ann.

Sean leaped up and in one continuous motion took hold of the back of his chair and swung it like a golf club. The wooden seat caught Miles square on his chin. He tumbled sideways.

Sean jumped on Miles, shoved him to the floor and yanked the pistol out of his grip.

Ann heard a noise behind her and spun around as Rafe barged into the room. Sheila, she noticed, was standing perfectly still, her hand clasped over her mouth to stop from screaming.

"Nicely done," Rafe Neilson said. "I'll take the gun." Rafe extended his hand and helped pull Sean to his feet.

Two other police officers whom Sean didn't know appeared at his side. One took Gail in tow, the other tended to Miles, who was groaning softly.

"Where did you get a tactical police radio?" Sean asked Ann, catching his breath.

"Rafe gave it to me on the night Gilda arrived. You've seen it dangling from my lanyard all week."

"You could have reminded me that you had it."

"How?" Ann said, wrapping her arms around Sean's neck. "Anyway, it was better that you forgot. You might have ruined everything by giving my secret away."

"You're the one whose face shows everything," he said.

"Are you going to hug me or not?"

"Not until I finish yelling at you."

"Why would you want to yell at me?"

"Didn't you think the man with the gun might get a tad upset when you told him you'd called the police and they were outside?"

"Now that you mention it, I didn't. All in all, I'm glad you were here."

"You're a complete flake."

"Uh-huh. I tried to warn you, but you wouldn't listen. Now it's too late. You're stuck with me."

"Yeah. I guess I am."

Sean took Ann in his arms and kissed her—long enough to lose track of the time.

FIFTEEN

Sean tapped his pants pocket and hoped once again that Ann didn't notice. Still there. He opened the door to Squires' Place and gently ushered her inside. They walked beneath the large banner that hung across the lobby: Welcome! Squires' Place is Under New (and Old) Management!

"I've never been to a small private party at a restaurant before," she said. "Imagine turning the entire dining room over to nine people for dinner."

"Hello! Our guests of honor have arrived!"

Sean cringed. James Defoe may have given away the game.

"Since when are we the guests of honor?" Ann said.

"Think about it. If you hadn't stopped the Haydens, I'd be back in Elizabeth City and this building would be a smoldering pile of ashes, topped with sixty fifty-pound sacks of roasted grits."

They moved into the dining room. Sean noted that four square tables had been arranged to create one long table that could seat nine people. The lights had been turned down, and the bright red-and-white decor seemed almost cozy and romantic.

Thank you, James.

"That's strange," Ann said. "We're the first to get here."

Sean nodded. That had been his idea. If he and Ann got settled first, there'd be less chance of another guest spilling the beans with a grin or a giggle.

He led Ann around the table so that they could read the place cards: Rev. Daniel Hartman, Lori Hartman, Sean Miller, Ann Trask, Rafe Neilson, Emma Neilson, James Defoe, Mimi Gallagher and Calvin Constable.

"Oh, no," Sean said, as he recognized the image on Squires' Place's newly designed place mats. It was Erin Squires Bradshaw's watercolor of the interior.

"What's wrong?" Ann asked.

"I don't like this illustration. It looks amateurish," Sean whispered.

"Says who? This is a sophisticated rendering. Had you taken an art appreciation course in meteorology school, you'd know that." Ann winked at him.

Sean groaned. Here was another topic he could no longer be judgmental about.

"We're here! We're here!" several voices said in quick succession. The other members of the party arrived, prompting a torrent of hugs and handshakes.

The door to the kitchen swung wide. James Defoe entered, pushing a cart stacked high with the restaurant's signature red plates and bowls. His red-and-white apron proclaimed, Eat My Grits!

Daniel raised his hands. "My friends, please join me in prayer. Heavenly Father, we have much to be grateful for tonight. We've lost our dear friend Richard Squires, but his legacy remains with us. James Defoe has come home to Glory. We ask Your blessings on his work—and also on Ann Trask and Sean Miller, two young people who have fallen in love."

Sean heard someone at the table giggle. Daniel ignored the interruption and continued. "We give thanks for our food today. Bless it to our use and us to Your service. In Jesus' name. Amen."

Sean felt Ann squeeze his hand. What, he wondered, would they all talk about during dinner that wouldn't give anything away? He decided to start the conversation with a safe topic. He raised his glass of sweet tea and said, "To James Defoe, the new—and old—manager of Squires' Place. May this Carolinian landmark continue to serve the best grits in the South."

"Why thank you, son," James replied, in a thick Southern drawl. "I hardly ever run into a silver-tongued Yankee. I suppose I'll have to get used to you."

Sean cringed again. He smiled as graciously as he could and said, "Well, North Carolina gets a good assortment of storms each year. I'm sure I'll be a regular guest for dinner."

James nodded—gratefully, Sean thought. "The door is always open."

Lori switched the topic back to Squires' Place. "James, do you intend to run the restaurant the way Richard did?"

"Why argue with success? Richard built a successful business. I figure, if it ain't broken, I won't fix it."

"That's what I wanted to hear," Emma said. "I'm happy to have a unique restaurant to recommend to my guests."

"Does that include using Richard's recipes?" Lori asked. "Including Cheesy Shrimp and Grits?"

"Of course I'll keep all the old favorites, but I want to expand the menu. I'm debuting two new grits dishes tonight. They were suggested by Calvin Constable, of course—Curried Grits and Grits Mediterranean Style, made with cinnamon and oregano."

"Curried grits are certainly interesting," said Mimi Gallagher. "It isn't a combination I've had before today."

Sean looked at Rafe across the table. They simultaneously mouthed *Yuk*.

"Enough about grits," Mimi said. "I came this evening to learn the skinny about a murder. Come on, Rafe, pony up the juicy details."

Rafe snorted. "I'm afraid the details are more dreary than juicy. Miles and Gail Hayden turned on each other in ten minutes. Each insisted that killing Richard Squires was the other's idea, and that the other did the actual killing.

"We're fairly certain that Miles hit Richard with a club while he was covering up the generator after fixing it. Richard was small and easy to lift, even during a hurricane. Both Miles and Gail carried him to the fallen steeple and placed him under the rubble while Sean was in the church getting help for Carlo Vaughn.

"This was purely a crime of opportunity. The Haydens didn't know if they'd get the chance to kill Richard that evening. They didn't know if or when he'd leave the emergency command center, but they were ready. They waited in their car, near Richard's, and followed him. The broken generator and the fallen steeple were enormous strokes of luck for them—and bad luck for Richard."

"What would have happened if Gilda had gotten worse?" Emma asked.

"The Haydens would have gone back to Squires' Place," Rafe said, "and waited out the storm. Gail and Miles felt safe in this building because it had survived several other hurricanes."

"The first time we talked to 'Sheila Parker,'" Sean said, "we were surprised to see piles of documents on his desk."

"That was Gail's doing," Rafe said. "After Richard was killed, she wanted to eliminate any paper trail that might show his intention not to sell Squires' Place. She admitted shredding copies of several letters Richard had sent to Miles turning down his offer."

Ann jumped in. "Gail told us lots of lies. It simply wasn't true that someone tried to sabotage the church's backup generator."

"No," Rafe chuckled. "But her phony claim got you going. That was the whole point—to make you think that someone else had a different motive for killing Richard."

"She also lied about her relationship with Richard," Ann said.

"There was no romantic relationship," Rafe said. "Gail Hayden worked for Richard and he brought her to Glory Community on a few Sundays."

"But what about the photograph in Richard's office? It depicts a loving couple."

"I'll let Lori answer that one," Rafe said. "She's now the photographic expert in Glory's police department."

"We took a close look at that photo and concluded it was doctored. The base photo was of Gail standing on the Outer Banks. Then Richard's photo—a happy shot of him taken somewhere else—was superimposed. The result was a photo that made them look like they belonged together."

"Every married man should keep that technique in mind," Rafe said.

Both Emma and Lori dug their elbows into Rafe's ribs. Sean peered at Ann. She looked pensive.

"Penny for your thoughts," he said.

"I prayed for the truth to come out, to convince people that I wasn't responsible for Richard's death. But now that we know the facts I can't help thinking how sad a story this is. I almost feel sorry for the Haydens. They're going to spend the rest of their lives in prison."

"Yes, they are," Rafe said, "and because we caught them, your reputation in Glory has been restored. I can't feel gloomy about that."

"Me, neither," Lori said. "I enjoyed seeing the *Glory Gazette* publish a detailed retraction of the first article they wrote about you, complete with an apology."

Sean nodded. "It would have been nice if Phil Meade had apologized to Ann as graciously."

"He expressed regret as best he could," Ann said. "Phil told me that he overreacted because Richard was a good friend, and he needed to blame his death on someone."

"That's probably as good an apology as Ann will ever get from Phil," Rafe said.

"That's okay," Ann said. "I've decided to forgive Phil. There's no point in holding a grudge."

"Some people find it hard to back up once they've traveled a while down the wrong road," Daniel said.

"Look at me," James said. "It took me twenty-five years to forgive Richard." The he stood up and asked brightly, "Who's ready for dessert?"

Sean's "Me!" began the chorus of eager replies.

James carried a large sheet cake from the kitchen. He placed it in front of Ann, who promptly burst out laughing.

"This is your doing," Ann said to Sean.

"Guilty as charged. I came up with the decorations." He leaned over and gave her a quick kiss on the cheek.

"Hand me that cake knife," Ann said. "I can't wait to make the first cut."

She tilted the cake gently so that everyone at the table could see the top.

To the left was the weather map symbol for a hurricane.

To the right was a quote from Scripture: "Forget the former things; do not dwell on the past."

In the middle was an image of Carlo Vaughn, reproduced in icing.

Sean heaved a deep sigh. "Isn't it a crying shame that Carlo can't be with us today?"

"Alas, poor Carlo," Mimi said. "No one minded him being a bit of a lady's man at the Storm Channel, but putting the moves on a vice president's wife was really foolish. Carlo is now our official 'reporter at large.' Last week he was in Phoenix, frying eggs on the sidewalk during a freak heat wave. And next year he'll travel to Alaska to report on the weather during the Iditarod dog-sled race."

Ann plunged the cake knife into Carlo's photo. "It won't be easy, but I'll try to put Carlo behind me."

She ate a piece of Carlo's image and flicked some icing at Sean. His grin made her stomach flip over, and it also filled her with sadness. Sean would soon leave North Carolina. Where did that leave her? In love with a man who lived almost six hundred miles away and would only return to Glory in rotten weather.

What a mess I've gotten myself into.

She glanced sideways at Sean. Their situation—the long-distance commuter romance—didn't bother him. He acted satisfied—annoyingly satisfied, as Ann saw it—with the way things stood.

One day soon, she'd have to kick-start him out of his complacency. They both needed to hash out the problem and decide their future. But not tonight. This dinner was a celebration. She wouldn't do or say anything to cast a shadow over everyone's happy evening.

Ann turned when Mimi Gallagher tapped her glass. She rose slowly, as befitting her elegant appearance. "Mother Mimi has an announcement," she said. "I am delighted to report that Sean Miller and I will soon be working together far more than we have in the past."

Ann's fork slipped from her fingers. What? Sean hadn't said anything about a new assignment that would involve him more with the Scandal Channel. Why would a meteorologist agree to such an arrangement?

Ann turned to face Sean. His grin had broadened to encompass most of his mouth.

Mimi continued. "I fear that I haven't communicated as clearly as I should have. Let me explain. A week ago, Sean Miller told Cathy McCabe, his boss, that he would be forced to leave the Storm Channel for personal reasons." Mimi emphasized the word *personal*. "Not wanting to lose such a valued employee, Cathy proposed an alternative. Because the number of mid-Atlantic hurricanes seems on the rise, Cathy has decided to base Sean in Glory, complete with his newly repaired broadcast van. He will cover hurricanes and other storms in Georgia and the Carolinas."

Ann was utterly speechless. She looked at Sean as tears began to fill her eyes.

"Because the winter weather in the Carolinas is not all that interesting, Sean will also be available to support remote broadcasts for the Scandal Channel. As I noted earlier, Sean will work closely with Mother Mimi and, in the fullness of time, may even learn to conduct interviews without getting himself into deadly peril."

Sean reached for her hand and held it tightly.

"Sean has been given his first assignment," Mimi continued. "He will produce a feature segment on the life and death of Richard Squires, which will appear both on the

Storm Channel and the Scandal Channel. I anticipate that Ann Trask will appear in said feature." Mimi smiled at Ann and took her seat.

Ann could only stare at Sean. But Sean's pallid face showed almost no emotion. If anything, he looked panicky. She poked him in the ribs and whispered, "If you don't start smiling, I'll make up with Carlo."

Sean released her and stood up. "I have an announcement to make, too." He cleared his throat. "In front of my new friends and new colleague, I want to state that I have fallen completely and hopelessly in love with Ann Trask. She is everything I could ever want in a woman and I can't imagine spending my life without her."

Ann put her hand in front of her mouth to hide her trembling lips. "Sean," she said. "I love you, too."

"There's more to my announcement, Ann. Please let me finish while I can still speak."

Ann heard Mimi laugh and Emma and Lori sniffle.

Sean knelt in front of Ann and fumbled for a moment to retrieve something from his pocket. "Ann, my love, I ask you before God, will you do me the honor of becoming my wife?"

Sean opened the small box in his hand. He slipped an engagement ring on her finger.

Tears slid down Ann's cheeks as she said, "Yes, Sean. Of course I'll marry you."

Sean got to his feet and helped her stand. Ever so gently, he put his lips on hers. Ann knew that the people around her were laughing, shouting and applauding, but they sounded very far away.

"Our wedding's not going to be on the Scandal Channel, is it?" Ann teased when Sean pulled her into a hug.

"Do you want it to be?" Sean laughed.

"I think I'd prefer the Storm Channel, actually."

"That's an idea. Maybe we should get married during the next hurricane. And Carlo can come down and cover it, and—"

"Just kiss me again, Sean Miller, before I change my mind."

"You got it," Sean said, and leaned in to give her the kiss of a lifetime.

* * * * *

Dear Reader:

Have you ever read one of those classic cozy mysteries written decades ago that show how past events can intrude into the present and cause chaos in people's lives today? We've always wanted to tell that kind of story, and *Grits and Glory,* our third cozy mystery set in Glory, North Carolina, gave us the perfect opportunity. Two of the characters are prisoners of their own past.

Ann Trask, of course, focused the lion's share of her attention on events that happened seven years ago. Perhaps she made a bad decision when she led a group of children into an old shed during a thunderstorm—or maybe she had no other choice. In any case, her preoccupation with the past impacted on both her shaky relationship with Sean Miller and her on-again, off-again relationship with God.

But Ann wasn't the only person who had to tear loose from the past. Richard Squires also had to restore a relationship with James Defoe that had been shattered years earlier.

In the Book of Philippians 3:14 NIV, Paul teaches that to "press on" and move forward we must forget what is behind and strain toward what is ahead.

Both Ann and Richard eventually overcame their pasts and therein lies the moral of our story. *Forgive, forget and press on!* When Richard forgave James, he was able to renew a precious friendship that he'd thought was beyond repair. When Ann forgave herself, she found love with Sean Miller and set the stage for a happy life in Glory.

We hope you enjoyed reading this third story about Glory as much as we loved writing it. We've planned our next visit to this charming Southern town just in time for Christmas. Plan to join us for dinner at the Scottish Captain, our favorite B and B. There'll be a chill in the air, decorations everywhere and a wannabe killer at our table.

DISCUSSION QUESTIONS

1. We are taught to trust God but Ann Trask was unable to do that. She preferred to trust herself and rely on her own abilities to solve her problems. Were you ever forced to trust God completely? If you were, what did you discover? How did it change your life?

2. Ann's past eventually came back to haunt her and she was forced to confront it. Has an event in your past ever haunted you? How did you deal with it? Were you able to move past the events?

3. We earn our reputations. Has anyone attacked you publicly and destroyed your reputation? What did you do? How was the matter resolved? Was your reputation restored?

4. Ann had trouble forgiving herself. Have you ever believed that you could never be forgiven for something you did? How did your belief in God's grace comfort you? Was it enough at the time?

5. Bullies can terrify us and make us feel weak and unloved. Have you ever been forced to face down a bully? Did you confront your bully head-on? Did someone help you? What was the outcome?

6. It's clear to Ann that Phil Meade didn't like her and his objective was to make her life miserable. He went

behind her back to harm her. Has anyone gone behind your back and discussed your past with others? Were you forced to defend yourself? How did you handle it?

7. We are told to work "as if for the Lord." Did you ever have a job that you couldn't wait to leave? How were you able to "work as if for the Lord" in such a job?

8. Ann loved her job, yet she was willing to walk away and find another job in another city. Have you ever been uprooted? How did you handle it? Was the decision to move yours to make? How did you react to leaving your friends and starting over? How did God guide you in your new surroundings?

9. Ann was attracted to a handsome face and quickly discovered there wasn't much behind that face. Has this ever happened to you? Have you ever fallen in love with someone who later proved unworthy of you? What made you break off the relationship?

10. Sean wanted to help Ann, but she was reluctant to accept his help. Has someone offered to help you solve a problem? Did you accept that help freely, or, like Ann, did you decide to go it alone?

11. We can't help who we fall in love with. Ann found herself falling for a man who lived in a different part of the country. The problem of distance seemed unsolvable to her, but Sean believed that God would make things right for them. Have you ever had a similar problem? How did you deal with it?

12. Ann and Sean felt they were right for each other, even though they'd only known each other a short while. Have you ever fallen in love without really knowing someone? Did you feel this person was someone God sent to you? How did it work out for you?

13. Church congregations often squabble over staff members. Have you ever been part of a congregation that disagreed about staff? How did your pastor handle the situation? What did you learn about your fellow brothers and sisters in Christ?

Love Inspired
HISTORICAL

INSPIRATIONAL HISTORICAL ROMANCE

Cowboy Kody Douglas is a half breed, a man of two worlds who is at home in neither. When he stumbles upon Charlotte Porter's South Dakota farmhouse and finds her abandoned, he knows he can't leave her alone. Will these two outcasts find love and comfort together in a world they once thought cold and heartless?

Look for

The Journey Home
by
LINDA FORD

Available August 2008
wherever books are sold.

www.SteepleHill.com

Steeple
Hill®

REQUEST YOUR FREE BOOKS!
2 FREE RIVETING INSPIRATIONAL NOVELS
PLUS 2 FREE MYSTERY GIFTS

Love Inspired.
SUSPENSE

YES! Please send me 2 FREE Love Inspired® Suspense novels and my 2 FREE mystery gifts (gifts are worth about $10). After receiving them, if I don't wish to receive any more books, I can return the shipping statement marked "cancel". If I don't cancel, I will receive 4 brand-new novels every month and be billed just $4.24 per book in the U.S. or $4.74 per book in Canada, plus 25¢ shipping and handling per book and applicable taxes, if any*. That's a savings of over 20% off the cover price! I understand that accepting the 2 free books and gifts places me under no obligation to buy anything. I can always return a shipment and cancel at any time. Even if I never buy another book, the two free books and gifts are mine to keep forever.

123 IDN ERXX 323 IDN ERXM

Name	(PLEASE PRINT)	
Address		Apt. #
City	State/Prov.	Zip/Postal Code

Signature (if under 18, a parent or guardian must sign)

Order online at www.LoveInspiredSuspense.com
Or mail to Steeple Hill Reader Service:

IN U.S.A.: P.O. Box 1867, Buffalo, NY 14240-1867
IN CANADA: P.O. Box 609, Fort Erie, Ontario L2A 5X3

Not valid to current subscribers of Love Inspired Suspense books.

Want to try two free books from another series?
Call 1-800-873-8635 or visit www.morefreebooks.com

* Terms and prices subject to change without notice. N.Y. residents add applicable sales tax. Canadian residents will be charged applicable provincial taxes and GST. Offer not valid in Quebec. This offer is limited to one order per household. All orders subject to approval. Credit or debit balances in a customer's account(s) may be offset by any other outstanding balance owed by or to the customer. Please allow 4 to 6 weeks for delivery. Offer available while quantities last.

Your Privacy: Steeple Hill Books is committed to protecting your privacy. Our Privacy Policy is available online at www.SteepleHill.com or upon request from the Reader Service. From time to time we make our lists of customers available to reputable third parties who may have a product or service of interest to you. If you would prefer we not share your name and address, please check here. ☐

LISUS08R

Love Inspired
SUSPENSE

TITLES AVAILABLE NEXT MONTH

Don't miss these four stories in August

THE GUARDIAN'S MISSION by Shirlee McCoy
The Sinclair Brothers
Heartbroken after a failed engagement, Martha Gabler
heads to her family's cabin for some time alone. But her
retreat soon turns deadly. With gunrunners threatening
her life, Martha has to trust undercover ATF agent
Tristan Sinclair to protect her—and heal her heart.

HIDDEN DECEPTION by Leann Harris
Elena Segura Jackson is frightened when she stumbles
upon her employee murdered, and she's terrified when
the killer starts vandalizing her shop. Clearly, she has
something the killer wants...but what is it? With Detective
Daniel Stillwater's help, can she find it in time to save
her life?

HER ONLY PROTECTOR by Lisa Mondello
All bounty hunter Gil Waite wants is to find a fugitive and
collect the reward. Then he meets the fugitive's beautiful
sister. Trapped in Colombia while rescuing her brother's
baby, Sonia Montgomery needs Gil on her side if she's ever
going to get herself and her niece safely home.

RIVER OF SECRETS by Lynette Eason
Amy Graham fled to Brazil to atone for her family's sins—
she never expected to discover Micah McKnight, the man
her mother betrayed. Micah doesn't remember who he is,
and Amy is too scared to tell him...but as danger escalates,
Amy's secrets could cost her everything.

LISCNM0708